THE EMPORIUM OF MANY THINGS

THE EMPORIUM OF MANY THINGS
BOOK 1

DAN LOWN

This is a work of fiction. Similarities to real people, places, or events are entirely coincidental.

THE EMPORIUM OF MANY THINGS

2nd Edition

Copyright © 2024 by Dan Lown

All rights reserved.

No part of this book may be reproduced in any form or by any electronic or mechanical means, including information storage and retrieval systems, without written permission from the author, except for the use of brief quotations in a book review.

Cover art by DLR Cover Design

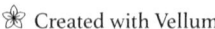 Created with Vellum

For my Mum

CHAPTER ONE

THE LAND SHUDDERS against the cold veil creeping along its skin. Shadows gather, unrelenting in their crawl, to plunge the world into oblivion. The festering carpet of beasts left in their wake spread their claws in the dank earth and shake off the grave mould. Reflective eyes in their hundreds awaken to the chill of the night across the valley floor, and just like that, the dwindling stain of humanity is beset on all sides by ravenous creatures prowling the night.

To the west, the sun gasps for air; almost buried alive by the darkness beneath the endless trees of the Everdark horizon, soon to be just another memory. In the east, quiet fires blink into life, desperate to stave off the shadows until the daybreak's relief.

The time has come for the people of Glimmer's Reach to retreat into their boarded homes, leaving their helpless militia to clamber atop the ramparts and palisade walls, their eyes wide with the fear of what they know will soon come to tear down their lives. Their village walls are a token plea for mercy, but it will not save them from the horror. They need help. And if they want my help?

They'll have to buy it.

The taste of autumn washes over my tongue as I coax my pipe into life. While I bask in the last of the day's respite, the sun's dying rays peek below the rolling clouds and cast their opaque underbellies pink with blood mist. Golden bars filter through the latticed porch wall of my home-turned emporium, the emerging pipe smoke swirling in the shafts of fading light. My chair creaks as I rock, looking out from my lonely hilltop nestled between the two worlds of glimmer and gloom... of bone-chilling fear and the unrelenting terror of the unknown.

Another smoke ring drifts lazily towards the drowning sun, its final smothered gasp lost to the snaking shadowed tendrils clawing across the land. Fire ebbs from the sky, giving way to the laughing moon perched high above the rolling clouds, gleefully awaiting the carnage to come.

Wolves howl in the Everdark, turning my gaze to the blackest nooks of the Shadowlands. That's the signal for this old man to open the shop that never opens, or so the denizens of Glimmer's Reach would tell any passers-by fool enough to listen. The children of darkness can afford an old man a moment's peace to savour the dying light, for the night is young, and what is life without a little pleasure? I pull on my bowl of autumn, stoking the fire within, the apple and cinnamon smoke seeping through my lungs like hard rain on the parched earth of a barren wasteland.

Perhaps tonight will be the night when I finally get a customer. One that isn't a meandering fool looking to buy seed and a bar of sodding soap.

Of late, only the brats of Glimmer's Reach have frequented my shop, pushing one another to approach the emporium in the false safety of the burning sun, but they never quite make it. They never dare. This place is not for their kind, and though they're typical idiot children for the most part, in my limited experience, kids often have a strong nose for places they shouldn't go.

No... In truth, I cater to a different type of clientele; one that I used to kill for a living. The scourge of this world has needs like any other, and where I once offered them release from their cruel existence, I now provide them with ulterior means to live; but truly, that is neither my problem nor my concern.

This is no charity. There is no good deed to be done here. My lips draw back in a sneer at such a ridiculous notion. I do not *care* for their wellbeing.

I merely enjoy the dangers of a previous life.

Another creak. Another drag from my bowl that tastes like spiced apple and autumn leaves. Another smoke ring.

I suppose retirement just didn't cut it for an old Blade like me, but that is not so uncommon in such circles. Few as we are, most of my kin unfortunate enough to deny the Shepherd of an early death go on to shadier vocations, their black and white views of the world severed by the cold, grey knife of reality. Maybe that's why I opened up shop right here, of all places. Or maybe this old bastard just wants one more roll of the dice before kicking the bucket for good this time.

A final drag and I tap the pipe against my heel before easing out of the chair, my old bones creaking like spent floorboards.

They say death is the end. If only that were true.

I take a ginger step towards my front door, muttering the appropriate curses of an old man as I flip the wooden sign.

"Open for Business."

Maybe tonight I'll make enough to keep this damn place open, but survival is always the top priority. The sign is written in old blood, one of the clues that I cater to more than just the babbling piggies of the nearby village and the roaming fools eager to see their guts ripped from their arses. I move to open the door, but a niggle in my mind stays my hand. Have the roses grown?

Peeling away from my sanctum, I frown at the patch of tilled earth along the edge of my porch and then ease myself from the low ledge, my hip flaring like always as I lean down to inspect the rising thicket of black briar. All around the house, herbs of reds, yellows and greens grow easily, swaying gently in the wind, their petals turned inwards against the cold of the long night.

All except the damn corpse roses.

The vines have crept, and their thorns are looking a little bigger. Carefully, I touch a barbed thorn with my finger. A razor sting draws fresh blood. Much sharper than last month too, but still they refuse to bloom. Sucking on my open wound before something else can, I brush the loose soil at my feet to one side, uncovering the dried husks of fish and rodents, their bodies dissolving beneath the acidic roots of the bush. For life, death is the best fertiliser. An old woman once told me that, standing in her verdant garden bustling with new life. And nothing could be truer for the corpse rose.

Still remember the moment I received them on our wedding day, a gift from my beloved wife, Silaea. A smile blossoms on my lips at the memory. I was surprised when she gave them to me, all smiles and laughter. Never had much use for flowers. All my knowledge was wrapped up in herbalism for medicine and poisons, but the corpse rose was different. They were exceedingly rare, and from a land so far away you could never hope to walk there in a thousand years. I've done my best to grow them ever since, but the bastard things wouldn't take no matter how hard I tried. She said they were stubborn, like me. At the time, I waved the notion off. Turns out she was bloody right.

I can still remember smacking my head upon the ground in frustration, having tried every trick from every tome I could find. Since then I've become quite the gardener, by all accounts, but despite my best efforts, the corpse roses never did flower. A lump gorges in my throat, cutting the oxygen from my lungs. Now, my love is no longer with me. I suppose it's become my dearest wish to honour her memory. To finally see them bloom.

"Rats," I mutter under my breath, wiping the mud from my boots. "Need more rats for the soil. Better set some traps after work." Or during, considering my current lack of customers.

I climb back onto my feet and head for the shop, pulling the old wooden door open and making it cry out with an angry crack of splintered wood. I shall not ease its suffering. It's my early warning system, though I confess it doesn't work for everything. Some of my potential clientele use forbidden passages not meant for this world. Not that I've had any of those yet. Only time wasters and flower pickers begging for a pitchfork up their arse.

Word travels slow around these parts, and I've got something of an awkward reputation to boot. Something to do with murdering everything that doesn't walk in the light. If only that were true. If I'm being honest, I've found just as many beasts living in homes and selling wares on the side of village streets as I have out in the wilds. The older I get, the less distinct the line separating man and beast seems to be. Perhaps I am just a jaded old fool, but something tells me I've managed to glean the sad truth. There are no monsters in this world. Only the dead, and those that are soon to be.

The door slams behind me to a *tinkle* of the brass bell, but I ignore it, instead stopping to admire my new floor. The ashen wood came all the way from the maddened valleys of Chitteren. Scorchwood, they call it. And nary a scratch on its pristine surface. Nor will there be, thanks to its almost demonic resilience, which holds doubly true when it comes to fire. Something I was sorely in need of up until now. I rub my hands together with glee.

"Excellent."

Candelabra burn low in the four corners of the room, piercing the inky darkness just enough to see the dark red bloodworm wooden counter cutting off the rear end of the room.

To my right by the doorway, a stack of parchment sits on a thin round table of wrought iron, detailing the various legal potions and remedies on offer, the ghost-white pages illuminated by the dripping red candles nestled nearby. Bit of a fire hazard, but what can I say? A kinky old bastard like me will do almost anything for a thrill. And besides, the rest of the building is made from old scorchwood too.

"Just ain't as pretty as my nice new floor."

Around the shop, shelves lining the walls bow beneath bottles every colour of the cosmos. Books and trinkets are stacked on one side. On the other, a collection of assorted weapons surrounds the great hearth of stone on the western wall. The last remnant of what stood here before my home transformed into the emporium where I stand. That hearth has warmed this great room for the best part of a decade. Now, maybe it will warm my customers instead. Or maybe I'll just get a badass brazier and light the room on fire. After all, what's the point of being fireproof if you don't stick your hand over a flame every once in a while?

The variety of weapons looks good hanging all around

the fireplace, from simple maces and swords to battle axes gored in the blood of innocents. It's a clever distraction, all very pretty for the fuck-wits waving their toy swords in the light of day. Daddy's little hero off to slay the troll, or what have you. Such people are not worthy of my true wares, and I always keep the real goods hidden from sight.

If you want those, you'll have to ask. And if you do, I might just cut your head off. This isn't some shop for a family visit. My real clientele is as dangerous as the night. Heck, they *are* the danger of the night. And I've got what they need.

Leaning on my good leg, I shift past the tables of mahogany and gnarled oak flanking the sides of my shop floor, cutting off space for customers to roam beyond my sight. I brush my fingers along the polished brass of trinkets and embroidered tomes left on display. Flashy, but essentially useless. Were it up to me, I would boil all the junk down and pour it over the pretenders. Make them regret ever wasting my time. Unfortunately, I've got to sell something legitimate amongst this firestorm of destruction I've amassed over the years, or I'm liable to bring the Inquisition down on my head. I hear they are prying bones from living bodies these days almost faster than the church can shove a collection box under their doomed noses. Think I'll leave them to it. I'm happier tucked away here and out of sight from the world.

I stop in my meandering sweep of the tables, picking up an ornately decorated curved dagger, its golden hilt encrusted with small emeralds. Pretty sure I bought this from a wandering merchant on the road somewhere down near Cragg Tor. Beside it, a similarly ostentatious lamp rests on a purple silk pillow. I drop the dagger with a *thunk* and scoop the lamp up instead, turning it over in my hand as I wipe away the dust in an attempt to jog my memory.

I bought this piece of shit from the same fool, who spun a yarn of the grandest palace in all the world, sealed by the Devil's right hand. He also proclaimed a genie resided within said wondrous palace, who was once enslaved to a sultan beyond the Kaghor Sands and could grant any wish. When I asked why he was selling such a useful item for so little coin, he simply twiddled his moustache and smiled. A good arm twist later, he told me the wishes came at too steep a price.

More likely, both pieces were forged along the Chain and were adorned with dyed glass, but I needed something to sell to make my emporium seem legit. Plus, I tested it out and even opened it up after getting the rusted chains off. There wasn't shit inside, but a palace of broken dreams. Made him throw in the pillow, which I'm pretty sure made it a worthwhile deal. Too bad I'm not interested in such trades.

Turning the fake over in my hands, it dawns on me that even back then, the idea of opening up shop was floating around in my head. I never thought I would actually go through with it. Just shows, you can't ever know what's around the corner. Or outside your front door.

"Stupid cheap crap." I drop the lamp back onto the pillow and move on.

Though I've delivered others from evil my entire life, such deeds carry no merit with the Justices of the Shattered Chain holding dominion beyond the Spinebreaker Mountains. So much as a single whiff of bad brew would warrant their march and bring them sniffing down upon me like bloodhounds, unyielding steel at their front, a contingent of heretic-burning zealots at their back with the unwavering surety of God on their side. It is for them alone that I maintain this front of a pathetic merchant peddling curious things. I cannot risk revealing my true trade to anyone with ties to the Chain. Far better to keep such nay-sayers and prying eyes from ever getting near my dark materials.

Or my throat.

The latched partition of my counter creaks softly open. I step through and lower it behind me, eying up an extra layer hanging on a nearby hook. Might as well put on my buckskin jerkin. Saves me burning through all the firewood before morning. And there should be plenty to keep me busy around the shop to warm these old bones.

I slide my arms through the jerkin, ready to receive the dark denizens of the night. So far, it hasn't been going well. I thought the flyers I distributed down in the village might have brought something in by now, but the monsters don't dwell in the village, so I took to pinning them on trees along the Everdark border instead. Ah well.

Feeling a little sorry for myself, I lean down and retrieve the leather-bound ledger resting beside an empty lockbox and dump it onto the counter. Peeling her open to the first page, I sigh at the neatly inked columns, the crisp parchment unblemished by the busy hand of a merchant doing good business. Though I cannot picture it for myself, maybe one day things will change around—

The thought ejects from my mind as the latch on the front door edges up, my heart quickening beneath my ribs. That sinisterly delicate touch. This ungodly hour when humanity hides beneath the furs, praying for salvation. It could only mean one thing. I swallow hard, slamming the ledger closed and stashing it below, scarcely able to utter the deadly truth stalking my emporium door.

"A real customer."

CHAPTER TWO

Candles flicker restlessly across my haven of gloom, their weakened sombre glow hopelessly trapped in the reflecting strands of silver web, all but consumed by ravenous darkness.

On the right side of the room, volatile potions bubble ominously on the shelves, bathing the eclipsed table below in a plethora of toxic violet luminescence and shifting hues of sickly verdant light. Trinkets of burnished bronze and fool's gold shimmer in the corrosive gleam, reminding me of the swamp witches of the Everdark, and their poisonous homemade brews.

To the left, moonbeams pour through the open shutter windows, creeping across the floorboards and up onto the tables like a malevolent spirit, phasing from this realm to the song of ever-rolling banks of cloud. Early in the night, when the moon sits at this perfect angle, its rays light up the gleaming facade on display for any and all who might come prowling, like a treasure horde of glittering silver burning bright in the deepest ruins lost to the passages of time. Should they fall for it, I'll know they are not truly worth my concern. And now is as good a moment as any to find out, for beyond the walls of my emporium, a visitor lurks in the moonlight.

I watch the front door creak open, my spine tingling with dangerous delight at the soft tinkle of my warning bell. The shade of an obscured face slips beyond the veil to gaze upon my sanctum of evil. Watching expectantly, my potentially first ever real customer eases onto the shop floor, clinging to pockets of umbra shadow and gliding on soundless footsteps. To give away the advantages afforded to me by the Night Mother, where swift death is dealt by hands unseen, goes against every fibre of my being. My target—or rather, my customer—edges between the tables, swerving candle and moonlit glow like their life depends on it. And maybe it does.

All manner of creatures hound the twilight, every one of them in search of something they desperately need. Mostly its food, or a place of relative safety to return to when the ire of day strikes hot over the mountain peaks. But sometimes, it is something more. Something sinister. That which only a festering mind plagued with ill-intent can conjure, in which only the choicest of dark materials can slake their unholy lust. That's where I come in. Once I was death's right hand. Now, I am his merchant. And I deal readily.

As the silver rays of moonlight depart once more from the mortal realm, the shade slips between the laden tables, the absence of their true form gliding over the worthless trinkets and polished armour littering the rough wood like a black velvet veil, never lingering, as though seeking something more... particular. Excellent.

Fighting the will to remain hidden, I grope the silver daggers stowed beneath my countertop. The twins are as beautiful as they are vicious. Lethal tools of a previous trade, bathed in the blood of human and beast alike. Once, they killed without a shred of prejudice, without a glimmer of mercy, all in the name of the lie we call "good". Now, they are my protectors in a new venture, one in which I hope not to require their service. And yet, despite my intent to keep them stowed, they call restlessly from beneath the bloodworm, thirsty to paint the shop in crimson splendour.

My fingers trace along the cold lines of their bodies, tingling with intent. I must remind myself that they shall not have their way. Not if I want to make this endeavour profitable. I've got some incredible wares to shift, but no vampire, murderer nor demon summoning librarian is going to talk commerce with a madman determined to sever their vocal cords at the first sign of business. I release the twins with a shuddering breath, steeling myself for the first of many encounters. I only hope my conversation skills are as sharp as my blades.

"Welcome," I call out, clearing my throat and giving away positional advantage. The shade lurking in the centre of the shop tenses. It snaps its attention to me like a burglar flushed from the shadows, caught in the traitorous rays of the moon's returning light. "Nice night."

Silence is my answer, and that may be all a simple peddler would perceive. I, on the other hand, have senses sharper than a headman's axe. Fear bleeds into the room, viscous and hot like a pulsing artery torn. Eyes sparkle from beneath night's veil, like a deer hunting the wolf beyond forest leaves, lost within the twilight embrace. I realise I am nestled in a pocket of darkness myself and have to will my feet to carry me from it. One does not dispel the habits of a lifetime so readily, but if I want this fiend to part with its money, I had better play my expected role. Familiarity with a twist of danger. That is what I must portray, lest they think

I am a fool to be preyed upon. I must remember *what* I am dealing with, rather than whom.

"Praise be the lord," comes a rumbling reply of a man, setting me on edge. That was not what I was anticipating, but simple words shall not lower my guard. I've seen every trick in the tome over my long years. Shit, I wrote the fucking thing.

The shade shifts closer, though still hides beyond light's touch. As he draws near, the silhouette keeps on growing, and I realise that which stands before me is less man than beast. At least in the size department.

"I, err... wasn't sure if you were open so late, only the sign..." my enigmatic guest trails off, glancing towards the door and back again. "Heh..."

"I am open," I assure him, drumming my fingers on the countertop, thinking. This customer proclaims light's grace, yet skulks under the cover of shadow. Perhaps he is cursed and seeks an ailment. Or perhaps his faith is a guise. A wolf in sheep's clothing seeking to gnaw the marrow from trusting bones. It matters not to me, so long as he doesn't assume me to be one of the flock. I've been called a black sheep more than once in my time, but that doesn't mean I'll so easily be reduced to cutlets. Such a notion makes my stomach growl. The shade of a man flinches in response. Hmph. Might have to pop down to the village tomorrow and buy some lamb.

The shade edges back. "That sounds like a big dog you have there, friend."

I can't help but smile at that, patting my stomach beneath the counter's cover for a job well done.

"Long as you play nice, he won't bite." I offer a placating hand. "But enough of that. Won't you step into the light? Friend."

The artery of silence bleeds anew, and an audible swallow reaches my ear. Is he hungry? The moon is full enough to unsettle the worgs, maybe even flush out a full-blown werewolf. He dodged moonlight like it was the devil itself. Perhaps, then, he seeks a cure.

"Yes, quite. Most rude of me." He edges forward, unsure, shifting into the lonely halo of warm candlelight burning atop my counter.

As his silhouette slides from the shadowed veil, the greasy skinned form of a man in brown, rough-spun wool takes shape, a chipped wooden cross hanging around his neck. He licks plump lips, his fleshy jowls of sagging skin quivering with each attempt to speak, as though invisible imps keep snatching the words before they can leave his throat.

I've seen it happen before, and while seemingly hilarious at the time, the afflicted had been trying to warn the village of an oncoming bandit raid. Needless to say, that little surprise put an end to the laughter faster than a blunt axe upside the head. This man looks like no bandit I've ever seen, and the imps are usually a lot more aggressive with their vocabulary-thieving antics. Still, a priest was certainly not what I had anticipated; and in my line of work, that's exactly the kind of bullshit you come to expect.

Standing across the counter from me, his sausage-linked fingers cling to his protruding belly, emphasised all the more by the coil of rope tucked below his midriff. His sparkly eyes shift unsteadily.

So far, the pieces in my head don't fit together. If he's alone, he shouldn't be here at this time of night, and I know he doesn't hail from Glimmer's Reach, nor the Everdark woods. Something doesn't sit well with me, making my fingers twitch for silver's surety. His nervous gaze sweeps over me like he's searching for something. Wealth, perhaps. Or strength. He's bigger than me, and I suspect he knows it. Although it won't do him worth a damn, but that's for me to know. My own gaze falls again to the priest's hands, his nervous fingers plucking absentmindedly, but still he says nothing. I can't help but pry.

"You lost? This here shop's in the middle of nowhere. How'd you find your way here?"

The priest in sheep's clothing bunches up, apparently uneasy with being grilled on something so simple. Very curious.

"What's the matter?" I ask. "Imp got your tongue?"

"Were that all it was," he replies with a meek laugh. "I, umm..."

He glances around at the surrounding darkness, trying to pierce the veil. "Are we alone, good sir?"

"We are," I assure him. "No one for miles but us, I would wager."

He seems to relax at that. An embarrassing situation perhaps, or maybe he likes the sound of an old man secluded on his lonesome in the dead of night. Easy target to be sure, and I wouldn't put it past a single one of these wayward bastards to make a move on my life. My fingers grace the silver tucked below out of sight once more, feeling the reassuring weight of it. Just in case.

"What can I do for you tonight?"

"Nothing you have here on display interests me," he begins, the edges of his mouth creasing uncomfortably. "I'm looking for something more... particular."

"I've got some rusty nails and a sack of old beans in the back."

His eyebrow raises at that, but I hold fast. I don't just dish out the real goods to anybody. Dealing with monsters is a dangerous game, but trusting humans often proves the deadliest game of all. For all I know, this guy could be a Chain enforcer.

"No, I'm not looking for beans. What I require cannot be bought in any normal shop."

"Then perhaps you're in the wrong place."

It's his turn to drum his fingers on the counter. He seems to think it over, wondering whether to divulge information that could probably see you hanged to a strange old man. Let's see if he's a gambling man.

"This may sound obscure, but I find myself in need of a..." he glances around again, before leaning forward to cover his mouth. I refuse to reciprocate, for doing so would put me well inside his larger-than-average striking distance, and you never know what lurks beneath the skin. His voice lowers to a strangled hush.

"... a cadaver."

"That right?" I tighten my fingers around the metal grip, my heart rate edging higher and my skin tingling with the thought of what was to come. Purveyor of goods, I may be, but I won't think twice about becoming the Blade I once was.

"Certainly," he says with a shrug. "I had heard you deal in shadier ventures out here from people down in the village. They told me to stay well away if I valued my soul."

"Did they now?"

"Indeed. God willing, you sound like exactly the kind of man I need. You, err... wouldn't happen to have a fresh body lying around, would you?" His gaze sweeps over me once more. Suddenly I begin to realise why. Very curious. Very deadly. I offer him a friendly smile, making the muscles in my cheeks ache.

"Fresh out."

He slumps a little, disappointment seeping into his joints like rigor mortis.

"Most problematic," he whispers, biting at his thumbnail. "Father Moyle will be most displeased with me. Ohhh, and to think I dragged the cart all the way up that evil hill as well. If I return without a fresh body, he'll…" The sentence trails off, but he's already said enough.

"That so?" I ask, still gripping the dagger tight. "What kind were you in the market for?"

"Hm? Oh, somebody old would be ideal for our purposes."

His hard eyes flicker over me for but a moment, a pause in his breath, then he returns inward, shaking his head. The cogs continue to turn in his mind beyond those sparkling eyes, his attention falling to rest on the counter's edge beside me. He drums his fingers on his chin, his brow riddling with creases.

"What kind of dog did you say you had?"

Alarm courses through me. This guy's built like an ogre, and judging by the writing on his face, isn't winning any subtlety competitions. The moment he finds out I'm shitting him, he's going to come down on me faster than an outhouse lid on a wet fart. I'm not what I used to be. Got to make the first move. I might only get one shot to survive this arsehole.

"Mongrel." I nod, dragging a blade from the hidden compartment beneath. "Big bastard. Watch yourself."

We lock onto each other for what feels like a lifetime. A silent war fought behind the eyes, where even a momentary twitch could tip the proverbial scale of lies and belief. My fingers ache from gripping the knife so tight.

His piercing gaze faltering, he leans forward to rest his huge hands on the counter.

"Let me take a peek at the little rascal—"

I jerk forward, burying the dagger sideways into his chest and puncturing a lung. He falters, blood bubbling wet in his throat as he spasms from the blow. His quivering hands knock the candlestick over and wrap around my neck with such speed, I fail to pull away in time. Closing seizure tight, his powerful grip expels the air from my throat and makes my eyes bulge in their sockets, the dark world turning wet with tears. Unable to escape, I wrench the dagger free and bury it in him anew, squelching through flesh and muscle. Trails of wet blood rip from him with every desperate stab. The resulting spray is hot on my face.

My attacker's strength wanes. He slumps over the counter with a hideous gasp and slides mercifully from my sight with a heavy thud onto the floor.

I also fall to the floor but behind the counter, banging my knees and gasping for breath, my vision swimming with colours in the black. That bastard was supposed to be my first real customer, too. Instead, he ended up trying to become my last. Bloody typical, that.

With fresh air revitalising my starving muscles, I claw my way up the compartments and lean on the counter, my hip aching like a son of a bitch. Across the shop floor, ghosts of moonlight phase back into reality, their interest piqued. I upturn the candlestick and peek over the other side. The priest in sheep's clothing stares lifelessly at the rafters, a thick pink tongue hanging out the side of his mouth like he's the one who was nearly strangled to death. I rub my neck, sure that it'll bruise. Don't even want to try talking right now.

Working my way to the hatch, I push up the partition and clamber through, moving delicately to the body and easing back down to my knees. The brown wool is stained black around his chest and stomach. A pool of pitch gathers beneath him in the low light. The dagger still protrudes from his chest, its blade shining with crimson lustre in the shaft of moonlight pouring through the window. I guess the twins got their wish. A fitting end for any monster, human or otherwise. Well, regardless of what he was, he owes me some damages. These days, I don't take shit for free. I've got to make a living somehow.

Patting him down, I glean something in a hidden pocket and trace my fingers across hot, wet blood for an opening. Inside, a coin purse jangles weightily. Something else is in there, too. It feels like paper. I relieve it from the pocket, the folded sheet tea-stained and edged with fresh blood. While peeling it open, I twist around onto my arse and use my would-be murderer as a more than adequate backrest. Once comfortable, I angle the page towards the nearby candle-light pouring over the counter's edge and squint at the fancy hand detailing the page.

Wendal,

I've enclosed the usual amount in the purse, plus a little extra to sweeten any difficult deals. We are in desperate need of that body. Plagues won't wait. Our faith is strong, but only science can truly safeguard humanity. And for Heaven's sake, make sure the subject is a female. Old is good, but at this point we'll take whatever we can get.
Be swift, and careful.

Your friend,
— Father Moyle.

"Female?" I mutter, blinking. I look behind me at

Wendal's ashen face, my lips pursing with rising guilt. But then what was all that crap about the dog for? Staring again at the letter, I realise there's something penned below.

PS — Ruffles misses you already. Use whatever's left to bring him back a tasty bone.

"Ruffles?" I glance back at Wendal, suddenly putting together a very different story in my mind. "Oops."

What's the likelihood that someone else will need a fresh body tonight? Probably sod all. Still, it's not my fault he acted like a damn loon. And who in their right mind asks to see the damn dog, anyway?

"Grah!" I cast the blood-stained letter aside in irritation. This was the last thing I needed tonight. Now I have to move this son of a bitch before the taint of blood soaks into the scorchwood. It'll turn everything with a nose away save for the sodding vampires, and who the hell wants to deal with them?

Reluctantly, I climb to my feet, then slide the murderous twin from Wendal's chest to wipe it on his robe. I'll need to act quickly and stash this bugger somewhere before the wrong person sees him. The cleanup I can deal with later; but first...

I pull the drawstring on the purse, dumping the contents into the palm of my hand. The five gold coins make my lips pucker with surprise. That's some serious change he was carrying; though considering his intentions, it's hardly surprising. I turn the pieces over, examining the chained stamps running through them. It seems people are worth far more dead than they are alive these days.

Moving back around the counter, I fish out the ledger and strongbox from underneath. It takes a moment to find the iron key in my pocket, which, despite having no money, always manages to take my breath away. My fingers grace the cold metal, and I pull it free and stuff it into the lock. The heavy lid opens with a whine, and I place the gold coins inside. It's a hell of a start, though I can't help but feel it was ill gotten. Might have something to do with the corpse on my floor. Whatever. I slam the lid closed and lock her up.

The key safely returned to my pocket; I move onto the ledger, opening her back up to the first page. Excited, I retrieve the stinkhorn ink and hippogryph quill, also residing in the space below the counter. I pop the lid on the jar and dip the quill, guiding its end to the page. It hovers over the parchment; the ink glistening poison black in the soft candlelight. My mind swims with conflicting thoughts. I so badly want to make an entry, but to do so would be a lie. I haven't sold anything. I murdered a dodgy bastard and looted his corpse. It's hardly the way I wanted to do business. Fuck it. Who cares? It's not like anyone would know... No one save myself. I grit my teeth, trying to will myself to make the sodding entry, but I can't do it.

"Fuck!" I kick the counter, making my toes ache like a son of a bitch. Throwing the quill down, I slam the ledger closed and fling it back where it belongs.

"Son of a bitch is right..." I'll make my first entry sure enough. And when I do, it'll be the right way.

More discouraged than I have been in a long time, I return the rest of the items to the shelf and head back through the counter. With my full attention now on the arduous task, my shoulders slump. I begin to roll up my sleeves, taking in the mess covering the counter and floor. I can't help but sigh.

"Gonna be a long fucking night."

CHAPTER THREE

Sweat beads my forehead with every agonising step as I yank the dead priest off my porch and onto the dew dappled grass, my laboured lungs shuddering misty breaths into the cold night air. The bastard must be thrice my size on a bad day. Throwing in the effects of dead weight and I'm really up shit creek without a paddle.

The smell of blood lingers all around me, filling my mind with flashes of darker deeds from another life. I shrug them off and release his corpse with a relieved sigh. Bunching my hands against the strain, I look out into the blacked-out world I once called my own. Burning bright in a dark sky, the laughing moon glares down upon me, its sickle smile fit to burst. Laugh it up, arsehole. Some day, you'll get yours too.

Puffs of wind roll ever westward from the eastern peaks, gracing my sweat-soaked skin in gentle waves of blissful relief. Down in the shadowed valley, clusters of astral moonshade glint in the darkness, their ghostly petals reflecting the lunar light back at the glassy lake of a glittering night sky. Nestled deep within that lonely void, Glimmers' Reach stands sentinel, a lost ship sailing to a forgotten world on a sea of stars.

This landscape is deadly, and yet despite it all, beauty still finds a way. I wish Silaea could be here to see this with me. I can picture her now, taking a cozy seat on this conveniently placed corpse, nursing a glass of wine, her smile burning bright like the sun. My chest tightens, wringing my insides out like a wet cloth. She was an angel. By the Night Mother, I miss her. Even now, after all these years, her spirit still haunts me... but no amount of whining will bring her back to my side. What's done is done.

Steeling my heart, I turn back to more pressing matters, only for dread to seep into my tired bones. I'm barely halfway to the fucking stable, and my arms are ready to drop off. I'll be damned if I've got the energy to make it the rest of the way. It only now dawns on me that I could have dragged his holy backside through the bedchamber and out the rear door, rather than coming all the way around. But then I would have 'essence of dead guy' covering the floorboards running past my bed, and the rich stench of blood has a bad habit of putting me deep under.

After a lifetime of swimming through death's mire, you get accustomed to the guts and the rot. Shit, some nights I find myself struggling to sleep without it. Were my wife still with me, I wouldn't mind a little corpse trail here or there running about the house. But now I'm alone, and I've got to keep my wits about me; so through the front door we go.

Resting on the grass nearby, a wooden cart with two wheels and no mule stands idle. The priest's body wagon, I suppose. Had I the strength of my youth, I would use it to ferry his arse the rest of the way. Far more likely, I would snap my back like a twig and join him on my front lawn for a visit to the afterlife. It's a tempting offer, but I'm nothing if not a pain in the arse, and I would so hate to go so willingly. Slow and messy. That's much more my style.

"Guess that only leaves me one option."

Taking hold of the bloodied wool robe with my aching fingers, I begin the arduous process of pulling Wendal's hefty corpse across the grass of my secluded hilltop, careful not to get too close to the sheer slope dropping down into oblivion. If I said I wasn't tempted to roll the bastard off the edge and be done with it, I would be talking more shit than the Pope himself. The beasts would probably tear the corpse apart before a few hours past, but if there's one thing I've learnt over my long years, it's that anything that can go wrong absolutely will. No... Better I maintain control and dispose of the body myself when the time is right. Not like anyone's going to mess with a boarded up old stable anyhow. And if they do, maybe I'll just add them to the pile. Give them the full service with a smile.

Sweat-soaked and dropping every curse known to man, I continue to drag my burden around the side of the house past the well and brothers of cinder, otherworldly trees of light and shadow entwined like rampant vines. Their leaves are in full bloom, but I'll be damned if I can see them in this light. I would settle for burying the priest here, were such ground not sacred to my Order. Only brothers and sisters of the Shattered Blade receive the honour of being buried beneath their spindled boughs. They say that the brothers ferry our spirits to a world of blissful content. A reward for all the shit and suffering protecting the undeserving populace of this ruthless life. It's probably all bullshit, but you've got to find happiness somewhere; and there sure as shit isn't enough to go around in this life, so why not in the next?

Quietly, while I yank the body on by, I wonder who will bury me. More likely my corpse will rot and fester in the sun, playing host to a plague of parasites, then only to be shat out by the wolves across the valley floor. Who knows, maybe I'll become my own tree when I die. It's a nice thought, but thoughts and reality are seldom witnessed holding hands.

Fuck it. I've grown so bitter in my old age; I would probably just poison the ground, anyway. Leech the nutrients from my neighbours and charge them double for a taste. That makes me grin. I'm such a miserable bastard, and I wouldn't have me any other way.

Finally, by the Mother's grace, I make it to my stable. I say my stable, and technically that's true, but it's probably stood here for more than a hundred years. Dilapidated and ready to collapse at a moment's notice, I'm not deluded enough to use it for anything worth a damn. Not sure I even want to venture inside, considering the decay, but I've got to stash this idiot before the wrong pair of eyes grace his blood-stained visage. Gingerly, and not without a pang of fear, I slide one of the damaged wooden doors open and peer inside, unable to pierce the eternal gloom. Fine by me. If something is staring back, I would rather not know.

"Come on then, you tactless twit." I growl, dragging Wendal a final length through the door and kicking him into the corner to be feasted upon by spiders and shadows. Hardly a dignified resting place, but I'm sure his god loves him enough to overlook it just this once. And if not, well, then maybe he should've prayed to a better one. My darling wife always said God was a prick, and if anyone would know, I've no doubt she would.

"Comfy?" I ask, half expecting a response. It wouldn't be the first time something wearing a corpse answered me back with a bit of lip. Fortunately for me, this isn't one of those occasions. "Good. Keep it that way."

I resist the urge to slam the door behind me to vent my frustrations, easing it closed instead. One well-placed fart could bring the whole building down on my head, and I didn't just bust my balls to snuff it here.

I drag my sorry arse back towards my sanctuary, longing for a good woman to take pity on me. Having said that, were she here, she would probably tell me to shut up and cook dinner. Just don't get them like her anymore.

Back in the emporium, it's as though nothing ever happened. The tangs of iron and blood still clot the air, but in the oppressive gloom you can hardly see the stains. Languishing on my countertop, I can't help but wonder if there isn't a better way to run things around here. That was likely my first and last customer for a fortnight, and in the meantime, I'll be stuck bloody stranded here at the counter like a fool on a roof without a ladder.

Surely I have something to ease the burden of running this place, if only I could think outside the box. Perhaps I should cast an eye over my most dubious wares, see if anything fits the bill. You never know what dark and insidious magics might double up as the perfect domestic drone. Hmm. Could be useful. Could also have disastrous consequences. But there would be nothing worse than standing here for a month straight just for the next moron to pass through my door to ask where to find the nearest outhouse. Fuck it.

Sold on the finer points of slave labour, I take up the half-eaten candle and slide into the hallway behind my counter. Veering left, I head down to the far end of the hallway where my stockroom looms like a loot hoarding monster, jealously guarding its treasure from all trespassers. I lift the latch and give the door a shove, bouncing off the old wood. Apparently, I'm a trespasser too; and in my own damn home. I don't bloody think so. I give it another barge of the old shoulder, immediately regretting the jag of pain lancing down my arm. Why did no one tell me old people had no fortitude? I would've made sure to croak it bloody years ago had I known. Now I'm too long in the tooth and would rather go on suffering, so I give the bastard door another shunt, shooting lightning all the way down to my elbow. Son of a bitch.

Reluctantly, the door gives way to a hail of clattering from beyond, and I slip into the belly of the beast so seldom seen. Nestled within, a monster fiercer than any god or beast lurks in silent slumber. A creature whose soul is so foul, it taints the very world around it. I swallow hard, allowing the candle to lead the way into the true heart of darkness where evil sleeps. If anything should get decapitated on entry, it should be the candle. I've got plenty more of those.

Once sure that no claws shall rake my face off, I shove my way deeper into the stockroom. The piles of crap behind the door cascade from my path, and the distant hopes that nothing volatile happens to be contained in that particular collection of shit bubbles in the depths of my mind. While holding the candle forward, I glean the crates and leather bags cluttering the floor on the edge of the halo's light. Cupboard doors hang open, spilling trinkets and black magics of yore like stinking innards ripped from a blasphemous stomach.

Dominating the room, a large round table sits in stoic silence, its great plane littered with various trinkets and scrolls strewn across its face. Those are the dark artefacts I have yet to investigate, catalogue, and stow away. Admittedly, I might have become a bit lazy in my old age. Turns out the closer death looms at your back, the less you care about being pushed over the edge of life into oblivion's awaiting arms. For all I know, one of those scrolls could harbour secrets dangerous enough to cleave the bleeding universe, but as I said, I'm old; so at this point, it's more everyone else's problem than it is mine.

A number of battered wooden chests sit in a row against the side wall, wrapped in iron fixtures and locked up tight. Pretty sure I organised those recently. Some five years ago, as it happens. Damn. Time really flies when you don't give a fuck. And speaking of, I'd better not arouse the beast, lest I incur their hell-tainted wrath.

Creeping a little deeper, the stone vase resting atop the dormant hearth's mantel steals my gaze. I can't help but swallow, taking in every harsh rune on its porous surface. Magic infused chains wrap around its curvaceous body, the skull-shaped stopper bottling its neck staring out to survey the room in quiet contemplation. Is it watching me? It's hard to say. Still, given the choice, I would rather not disturb it. To call it a temperamental nightmare would be a gross understatement, even on the best of days.

A crackle of magenta energy skates across its surface, chilling me to the bone. I've got to move quickly.

Rifling through piles of assorted crap, malignant tools of destruction slide and scatter. Hurting these arseholes is the opposite of what I'm trying to achieve, but I would settle for something that can assassinate their coin purses without a trace. Knowing my luck, I've probably got just the very thing and will never know it.

"Aha."

I grin, gripping a brass leg protruding from a collection of mysterious metals and unreasonably sharp flints of reflective jade. I pull the leg free, revealing not what I had hoped for, but instead an old-looking lantern with frosted glass. A pale blue flame dances innocently within, lighting up the surrounding space. Burning soul-bright, the flame begins to swell, edging closer to the tightly sealed door.

Were my memory not fresh from the last incident with this thing, I might've been tempted to open it. But the innocuous flame residing within is no flame at all. It is a ravenous beast that feasts on the very air. Unleashed, its blaze would spread as far as the heavens, and most likely starve the entire world of oxygen; or at least that's what the nutter I relieved it from was raving about in the crypts. Despite having a particularly bad day at the time, I'm glad I didn't humour him. To say that this thing is dangerous is bloody laughable. It's nothing short of complete and utter world suicide. Well, everything, save that which lives underwater, I suppose; but who wants to live down there?

Drawing the trinket closer, the flame dances before me, as though willing me to grant its release. Like fuck. I should really put this thing somewhere safer than in crap pile number seven, and so I place it on the nearby wooden unit out of harm's way.

Working a little deeper into the room, I brush my fingers over a row of crusty silk-bound scrolls on the side table, wondering if a spell could be the answer. Perhaps a familiar of some kind, though how I would get such blatant black magics around the normal folk and Chain loyalists, I don't know.

"What's this?" I nudge the scrolls aside, causing tiny crackles of necrotic power to numb the tips of my fingers. Underneath, a small mirror lies face down in the dust, its tarnished wooden back raked with sharp scratches. Unable to remember where I acquired it, I draw the candle closer to glean the jagged scribble, while blowing years of dust from its surface. The musty cloud hits me in the back of the throat, making me splutter into the crook of my elbow. I need to keep the bloody noise down. Fortunately, I don't seem to have disturbed the beast... yet.

Turning back to the mirror, I flip it over and realise its face is covered by a dirty rag. I push it back, unleashing a hideous sight. It's me, and what of it? Even chiselled good looks are eroded by the winds of time. That dark and dirty charmer's still in there somewhere, lurking beneath the surface and ready to slay yonder tavern wench's less than exemplary virtue. Not that I ever would, I hasten to add. Even with things the way they are now, my wife would nail my balls to the bloody wall.

For reasons beyond sanity, I venture a smile, but my reflection hardly moves. Hmph. Can't say I'm surprised. I'm a dealer of vicious death and wanton magics, not some fucking clap-happy circle-jerker handing out a good time. I grimace at the unwavering face of scorn, and to my horror, it smiles back at me.

"Ah!"

I drop the mirror; the handheld tumbling over end and bouncing off the darkened floorboards. The fuck was that all about? Slightly more shaken than I would like to admit, I kneel down to retrieve it. The halo of candlelight reveals the image of my face staring through the mirror into this world, the eyes shifting with intrigue. It makes me shiver with alarm. That's no bloody reflection I've ever seen.

My jaw falls slack as I witness the reflection reaching up into the real world. It places its withered hands onto the floorboards and leverages itself out, like it is climbing up out of an undersized trap door. The change in scale when it slides its torso through the mirror's rim plays havoc with my depth perception, but that's a bleeding footnote compared to the more prominent list of burning questions plaguing my mind.

"The hell is going on?" I growl, stepping back in the wake of my reflection dragging its legs through the tiny mirror, grunting and foul-mouthing like a seasoned pro.

"Son of the town's... favourite whore!" my double spits, pulling its last foot from beyond the veil and grabbing at his hip. "I'm getting too old for all this crawling about crap."

Singing to the bloody choir. I watch in awe as my doppelgänger rises to his feet, brushing dust from his simple—and identical—clothes, and sweeping back a mess of dishevelled grey hair. He's a good-looking son of a bitch, but nothing quite passes for the real thing. Admittedly, I'm not sure anyone else could tell the difference.

"What are you?" I ask, still somewhat bewildered. I can't tell if this is magic at play or some kind of creature mimicking me.

"I'm the only backup you've ever needed," my double says, readjusting his jerkin and taking up an unlit candle before stepping towards me and holding the wick to my own, the tiny flame creating its own double to complete the look.

"You think any of this shit is going to do you a favour in life?" he carries on pointedly, looking around with disdain. "Only person you can count on is yourself."

Amen.

"And if you need proof," he adds, stabbing a sagely finger past me towards the hearth, "just take a look over there."

A malevolent flare illuminates the walls. My muscles tense and I whip around, my heart rising so high into my throat that it threatens to choke me to death. I've half a mind to let it, rather than face the demonic ire that was stirring at my back. Across the cramped room, magenta light blooms beneath the vase's now shifting surface. A flourish of fiery script ignites on the once solid stone, turning my mouth dusty dry. I flit my gaze across the materialised words. The message leaves nothing to the imagination.

"Get. Out."

"Ah, shit," my double whispers behind me, snatching the words from my mouth.

Shit is right. I need to keep this short. Maintain the brittle peace tempered over so many years of painful coexistence. I part my lips, my mind racing for the right words.

"First thing you've said to me in bloody years." I growl at the volatile glow. "Must be getting soft in your bitter old age."

What the fuck is wrong with me? Do I have a sodding death wish, or perhaps a spare pair of bollocks in the bedchamber drawer? I look back at my double, who just shrugs and shakes his head.

"Can't say I would've done any better, champ."

The vase shimmers for but a moment, the unyielding stone flickering dangerously translucent. Within its swirling depths, unblinking golden eyes simmer like the surface of the sun, scorching hot and trained to kill.

I swallow again, but only salty fear slides down my throat.

Another jag of magenta energy ripples along the vase's chains, and the pressure in the room dropping to an icy low. It's time to get the hell out of here.

Wasting no time, my double and I dash for the hallway amidst the growing storm of vengeful light. We slam the door behind us and duck out of the way when something bangs against it, crackling with disbursed energy. That was too close for comfort, but had I really crossed the line, the hallway would already be painted in brains and shit. I wipe my brow, wondering what else this night can throw at me, only to remember it already has. I turn back to my double, who looks at me with a curious gaze.

"You look like you could use a lie down," he says.

"Pfft. That'll be the day," I shoot back. "I've got a shop to run. Crap to inventory, cheese to eat."

My double licks his lips at that particular morsel of information. "Well, that's what I'm here for."

"Eh? You are?"

"Course." He shrugs again, giving me a rare smile. I say rare, because I don't bloody do it. Probably bad for the cheeks at my age. When you're as old as the hills, it's best to make like them and refrain from too much movement. Got to conserve life in this lingering corpse where I can find it.

"It's like I said," my double goes on, "only person you can rely on is yourself. So why don't you go take a break, and I'll man the counter."

"Wh—what?! You mean, you would actually do that?"

"Who else is gonna do it? The rats?"

Interesting. I hadn't foreseen this. Were it a true copy, it would've surely told me to go fuck myself sooner than lifting a finger. And yet, here we are. Can't say I'm complaining. Not yet, anyway.

"Well?" he asks. "What do you say, champ?"

"I... guess that's okay. But I'm very particular. I don't just sell to anyone, you know."

"No shit. We're not trying to run a normal business here. We're shifting black market goods. I won't give the game away."

Very interesting. It can't hurt to try, can it? What have I got to lose?

"Yes. What have you got to lose?"

"Ah—Hmm... Indeed. Very well. There's—"

"Knives under the counter, and I'll holler if I need anything."

I blink at that. "How do you know all this?"

My double fixes me with a rising eyebrow. "I'm you, remember?"

"Right…" It's a little disconcerting, but I can't fault him. And there's no one less likely to stab you in the back than yourself. If it really is yourself. I guess only time will tell.

I shift uncomfortably on the spot, wondering just how deep this rabbit hole goes.

"You're not reading my mind, are you?" I can't feel the telltale signs of an invasive presence, but that honestly doesn't mean shit.

The double laughs, tapping his temple. "Why would I need to do that?"

"Right." I guess we could do a trial run, were we ever to get another customer, but around here, such things are few and far—

The doorbell tinkles from the main room and both of our eyes widen. I lean around the hallway door to peer onto the gloomy shop floor. It can't be, but it is. A customer! I glance back at my double, whose grimace creeps into another smile.

He rubs his hands enthusiastically, filling me with a disconcerting sense of dread. "Time to go to work."

CHAPTER FOUR

Blowing out my candle, I duck and roll through the open hallway door and swoop low beneath the bloodworm counter, praying the sparkling ghosts of moonlight drifting through the open-shuttered windows cover my advance. My hip flares with raucous complaint, joints creaking and elbows crunching with the strife of old age, the tax of a thousand wars weighing heavy on this battered battlefield the kids call "old man".

Despite my ever-growing list of weaknesses, enemies continue to beset us on all sides, forever ready to drag us beneath the surface into watery graves. Though I may be broken, I am far from beaten. I've got a job to do, and I'll be damned if anyone's going to stop me from doing it. It's time to make some goddamn money, and ink the first page of my ledger. Such a thought rouses the flames of youth, and before I know it, the aches and pains are melting beneath a riptide of fire-soaked adrenaline.

Somewhere on the other side of my emporium, my target of commerce looms. I can hear their feet shifting on the hard scorchwood floor and smell the fetid waft of malicious intent on the air. Well, if they think they can rip this decrepit old geezer off, they're in for a nasty surprise.

I flick my attention to the silver sword stowed in the long slot beside me, my true weapon of choice when shit really gets stuck between my teeth. A blessed concoction of runic alloy, that sword was passed down to me by my master—in a manner of speaking—and has seen me through decades of blood and guts, of horror and heresy. The fouler the beast, the deeper it cuts, and the wounds never close. Should my assistant have any problems, I'll not hesitate to unleash its destructive power. Such a relic will send even the toughest creeper running through the valley, and that goes double for anyone of the blood-sucking variety.

My back pressed to the cubby-holes below my counter, I realise just how many cobwebs are down here glistening in the quiet folds of the night. Layers of dust cover the unoccupied spaces, the outlines of items once stowed evident, their now empty voids sitting thus far untouched by the inevitable hand of grime. Even my damn cheese board is getting covered in filth, and I'm not talking about a finely aged wedge of naughty Saint Mullen. Maybe I should take a cloth to this son of a bitch some time. Or better yet, maybe my new assistant should. Now that sounds like a plan. A pang of fear trickles into my gut, making me gulp. I wonder if he likes cheese.

Right on cue, my double steps up to the plate and places his candle on the counter, ready and willing to take a knife to the neck in my stead. What a sight that would be, watching yourself bleed out on the floor before your very eyes. Must be surreal. I glance up at my new friend, and he looks down at me from the corner of his eye, a relaxed ease in his stance, his weathered hands clasped loosely behind his back. Here's hoping I never have the pleasure.

"What can you see?" I whisper, so as not to be overheard. There's no telling how close the target is.

My assistant makes a low, sweeping gesture with his hand, indicating he can't see shit. Who knew communicating with yourself was so damn easy? It's like he gets me. Like he *is* me. Still not sure how I feel about that notion, but I'd be lying if I said I wasn't coming around to the benefits. Just got to see what he can do when the time comes. Most men can readily give the lip day and night, but when it's time to cash in that mouth money, many fall apart like pissed-on parchment. If my double is anything like me—and I'm starting to suspect that he is—that won't be an issue.

With my attention locked on my assistant for signs, I rise towards the counter's edge, ascending the depths of shadow's grasp to risk the cheekiest of peeks. Beams of moonlight flood through the windows, illuminating a slender figure hunched in ragged clothes. Their focus is split by the baskets of dried herbs, their steps slow. They pore over one of the tables, lifting shaded ornaments and sniffing them peculiarly, before moving deeper into the emporium. It seems they are searching for something. Could be my lucky night.

"Might I help you with anything on this most auspicious night?" my assistant asks out of the blue, lighting a fire under my arse. I duck out of sight as the potential buyer swoops around, their fingers baring like claws. Did they see me? Surely not. It takes a concerted effort not to reach for the silver, but my assistant's unchanged posture stays my hand, his dubious smile returning.

Wary footsteps echo across the floor, drawing closer by the second. My heart rate quickens, and I have to force it to remain calm. To the discerning blood hunter, such a lack of arterial control would seldom go unpunished. Did I give myself away? I don't know what I'm dealing with here. If only I could see what's going on up there.

"I'm looking for something," comes a low husky voice, female, if I'm not mistaken, and much to my surprise.

As though reading my mind, my double lifts the back of his buckskin jerkin and slides the mirror from his breeches, holding it out for me to take. Of course. Why didn't I think of that? Now I just need to figure out from which angle to use it.

Peering into its reflective surface, I double-take at not my own outrageously handsome visage, but the face of a young woman, her tired eyes feral with distrust. What am I seeing? The view swings away from her to staring down behind the bloodworm to focus on an old man gaping into a mirror like he's seen a bloody ghost. The sudden swing makes my head spin, and I glance up to see my assistant watching me. He turns back to his customer, and I return to the mirror. The girl in front of the counter shifts her eyes uneasily, questions forming in her mind.

"Spiders," my double says casually, attempting to ease her nerves. Though somewhat youthful, she has a rough face, weathered by hard times and harder deeds. She's a killer. I know the look. Know the smell. Of cloyed blood and old sweat that lingers on the skin. Although it could just be the pool of blood beneath her feet. I tried to wipe it up before dragging the priest to his temporary resting place, but I wouldn't call it spotless by any means.

The girl shifts on the spot, her boots sucking with a sticky film. She doesn't even bother to stare down into the gloom, instead fixing my assistant with an accusatory stare. No words needed. Just two killers secluded in a dark room, and one big surprise if she decides to pull anything fast.

She scratches at her arm, raking blackened fingernails

over her dark stained tunic, her eyes shifting warily, until finally she sinks away from the candlelight. The air becomes heavy, and my heart rate looks to rise anew. My fingers yearn for the hilt of my sword, but my assistant holds out a placating hand. Is he mad? She's not here to bargain. Opportunist. Thief. Murderer. Her poison matters not. Only that it doesn't spread to infect our lives like it already has hers. She scratches her arm again, an infernal itch that does not seem to sate.

"Dust," she says suddenly, her voice harsh. So that's it. Powder scraped from the lunar dust moth's wings, mixed with acid and distilled into tiny crystals. It is a corrosive concoction that addles the mind and feeds the soul lies of warmth and contentment. Once locked in its hold, few escape its grasp. Dark alchemists make a killing selling the stuff, as it requires a surprisingly delicate hand to create. Get it wrong, and the effects range from ineffective to dissolving your insides. And don't get me started on sourcing the main ingredient. All well and good, but does my new friend know any of this?

"Sorry," my assistant says, his voice calm like spring's breeze. "I don't deal in that kind of medicine."

A gulf of silence consumes us. Her breathing intensifies, though she fights to contain it. Her hand rises to her arm's side once more, scratching like a phantom limb of which she has no awareness.

"They said you sell things no one else has."

"They are wrong."

Her nostrils flare, and her spare hand vanishes into her pocket. My own darts for the hilt of the sword, but my assistant bends below the counter and catches my wrist.

"Let me see here," he says, waving a stern finger at me. I blink in awe, wondering what kind of death wish he has. It's obvious she's about to take him for anything that can be fenced later down the road. He reaches into one of the cubby-holes, and I snap back to the mirror to see what he's up to, but he's already rising to meet the girl's startled stare. She bunches up, her frown descending to a soul grimace. She pulls her hand free, making the hairs on my neck stand on end.

"Here, take it." She snarls, throwing a handful of copper coins onto the countertop. "Is this what you want? All my fucking money for a hit, you tight-fisted bastard?"

I cover my mouth to quell the sigh of relief, surprised at the turn of events. I thought for sure that she was about to…

My assistant simply gazes down at the coins and sighs, too. Curiously, he begins stacking them into two piles; one twice the size of the other. He slides the larger stack across the counter towards the girl and pockets the lesser.

"One moment," he says, exposing his back to her hateful gaze. He moves along to the end of the counter, stepping over me in the process and mumbling about bloody spiders, then turns to the end cupboard where I keep my dried roots and powders. He collects a few items, then closes the cupboard door and steps back over me, returning to his spot across from her.

I stare into the mirror, trying to see what he has. Powdered scrub-thorn, root of cinder, and some dried saraca leaves? The properties of such ingredients twist and combine in my mind as I try to discern their purpose, and I have to refrain from slapping my forehead. Of course. Why didn't I think of it?

My assistant places the items on the counter before the young lady, luring her from the darkness like a fever drawn.

"The fuck's that?" she spits from across the counter, eying the items.

"Steep the leaves and root for fifteen minutes in steaming water once a day. About a cup's worth should do. You'll get about three doses out of it."

The girl shifts uncomfortably, edging closer across the sticky floor. She nods at it, still wary. "What's it do?"

"It should help calm your symptoms. Give you a chance to find what you're looking for. Alternatively, you can come back here and buy some more medicine. Do this for a month, and you might just kick the habit."

Her shoulders bunch with disdain, only to fall like weighted stones. Reluctantly, she steps forward, scooping up the copper coins and ingredients. She stares at the twine-tied leaf of powder.

"What's this one for?"

"Anti-septic," he says, pointing at her arm. "For your sores."

She stops scratching, suddenly aware, and puts her hand down. "I don't have sores," she corrects him, and bitterly at that.

"Glad to hear it. Take care of yourself out there."

"I—" She swallows, her eyes softening. Almost wet in the candlelight. "Th—Thank you, mister."

I look up at my assistant in awe, who just nods with an easy smile when she turns away, her footfalls heavy as she runs for the door and exits with a tinkle. I don't believe it. The son of a bitch actually did it. More than that, he thought outside the box and made a worthwhile sale where there otherwise wasn't one, and kept his guts in his stomach to boot. I'll be damned.

"There now, that wasn't so bad, was it?" he says, turning to lean on the counter and wink at me.

I rise from hiding with a stiff grunt, my words abandoning me.

My assistant reaches into his pocket and fishes out the copper coins, placing them on the counter.

"We need to fill out the ledger," I say with fervour, excitement invigorating me. Finally, I did it. I made a profit!

My assistant gives me an easy nod and reaches into the partition beneath the counter, bringing out the book, a pot of stinkhorn ink and a hippogryph quill. He opens the ledger to the first page and casts his gaze over the carefully written out table of contents in which no recording has been made. No longer.

I watch with abated breath as he dips the quill and begins scratching out notes in the appropriate fields. Date, items, profit made.

"Let's see here," he mutters, adding a new column on the far side of the page. He finishes scratching and places the quill down, walking past me for the partition as I slip closer to the ledger. I glance down at the page. Four copper coins added to the list. What a marvellous sight. Looking to the margin, I see what he added. BG2. I blink at that, cogs turning. Initials. My initials. His sale. I swallow dry, my stomach turning. Of course, it was his sale, I haven't done anything. My fingers tighten into fists, my excitement dashed. Shit. I can't even pull him up on it. He's bloody right.

I glance up at the sound of wandering footsteps to see my assistant striding across the shop floor to the front door. In my confusion, I call after him.

"Where are you going?"

My assistant turns confidently to face me in the shifting moonlight, still smiling. "Gonna make sure she gets on her way all right." He points a finger at me, his nail glinting in the silver light. "Full service, remember?"

I point back at him, unable to contain a smile of my own. "Full service."

My assistant nods, slipping the front door open and vanishing into the night with a soft clunk. I return my attention to the ledger, my stomach twisting with knots. I branded her a killer, and I'm probably not wrong. Only difference is I would have cleaved her head off and lost the damn sale. I've got a lot to learn, but I can't let that stop me. I will get my own sale, even if it bloody kills me.

Irritated with myself, I slam the ledger closed and return it to its shelf along with the ink and quill, when I notice one of the twin daggers is missing from their perch.

"The hell?" Looking around, its sister is nowhere to be seen. My gaze settles on the front door. Did he take it? I snatch up the mirror and stare into its revealing depths, gleaning that which my assistant sees. He's talking to the girl outside. She smiles, nodding as he points into the distance. I can't hear what they're saying, but she seems satisfied. I relax, feeling like this is really going to all work out. What are the odds? I decide not to consider it. It is what it is, and that's just fine by me. This old man could use a little lie down. I'm sure my new assistant can handle things for me.

I make for the hallway when something catches in the back of my mind, turning me back around to the silver twin resting silently below the counter. Drumming my fingers on my leg, I move to take it, tucking it in the back of my own breeches. Just in case. Satisfied, I head for my bedchamber, ready to take a well-deserved nap.

I've got a feeling everything is going to work out just fine.

CHAPTER FIVE

A world of restless dreams scatter to the distant tinkle of the doorbell, its high-pitched jingling wail snapping me awake in a confused haze. I grab at my arse for the twins, only to find the one stashed in my waistline. That also confuses me, but then the fog corrupting my mind begins to clear, unveiling the night's prior events.

Across my bedchamber, beyond the pair of leather chairs, the hearth burns with a weak flame. My woodpile reserves are running dangerously low, and I find myself more in need of coin than ever. It's no way to go into winter, and has become a serious motivator for making some fast cash. What's the point of surviving a life of battling monsters in the shit, only to die to the cold? The thought is unnerving. I'm too old to be dragging logs up onto this godforsaken hill, and the trees peppering the valleys are tougher than old boot leather.

My good friend, Marston, down in Glimmers' Reach, said I'm welcome to stay with him and his son Rob through the rough winter. Share the warmth of a good hearth. But I'm too damn stubborn to accept such a gracious offer. My entire life, I've fought tooth and nail for everything I've ever owned. Much as I would like to roll over and accept the easy path, it just isn't in my nature. So close to the end, I have no choice but to make my own way. If the cold is to take me, then it'll be with me standing on my own damn feet atop my hill, my frozen middle finger a parting gift to the world. The corner of my mouth curls at that. There are far worse ways to go in this life, and I've already had my fill of a good time. What will be, will be.

Throwing the furs aside, I lean forward and grab the mirror resting on the bedside table, peering into its uncertain depths. I frown at what I see, which isn't a lot. Darkness, grass, and tired palms rubbing against the chill in the silver light of the moon. I don't know what my assistant is doing outside, but what I do know for certain is the shop floor is unmanned; and that's more than enough to get me out of bed. I throw my legs over the side and rise to my feet, slipping my boots and jerkin on to shield against the shivers crawling along my skin. Can't help but wonder if we've had any more sales.

Eagerly, I cross the bedchamber and slip through the hall, stepping out behind the counter to look out across my empty shop. The ghosts of moonlight have shifted from the tables, now residing by the front door and lingering on the array of different coloured potions on the far end of the shelves, their contents vibrant in the pale ghost-light. Remarkable, how strong the moonlight is away from the fires of villages and towns. Out here in the sticks, it might as well be the bleeding sun.

To my elation, the ledger is resting on the countertop, which is not where I left it. Unable to contain my curiosity, I peel back the cover to the first page and run my finger down the sales column, my jaw falling slack with surprise. Two more entries have been entered into the log, and a note in the margin that reads "purse?". I raise an eyebrow at that. There is no doubt that my new assistant has been busy while I've been sleeping. He sold my last vial of whisperfang anti-venom for a piece of silver, and after that, a few bunches of dried rosemary and ragwort for two copper a piece. It all looks above board, but the true tell will be the contents of my safe.

I fetch the key and pull out the strongbox, placing it on the counter and levering it open to peer at the tiny stacks of coins inside. Well, what do you know? It's all there, down to the last copper. I close the box, a warm feeling filling these old joints with the quiet satisfaction of relief. I drum my fingers on the cold lid, somewhat dazed by disbelief. This is really working out.

Now if I could only find my damn pipe. In the absence of a musky leaf hit, I might have to settle for a cheeky drink instead. I've got some good stuff left over from that trip to Murkwood. Tastes like a horse's arse, and kicks like one too. Or at least that's what the seller told me. And judging by the huge black bruise he had on his shoulder and the unidentified crusty brown residue matting his beard, I would say he knew what he was talking about. Could hit a snifter right now, but I'm concerned about where my assistant has gotten to. I return the box and key to their rightful places and meander across the shop floor, sticking my head out the front door and staring into a chill breeze rolling off the shadowed mountains cape across the valley. Neither hide nor hair. Guess I'll man the floor myself for a while.

I shove the door closed with a rattle and ignore the jingling wail. Then I about turn and consider checking the tables for anything out of place, when a trickle of alarm needles down my back like a footpad in a dodgy alleyway that doesn't know the meaning of boundaries. I wheel back around, catching sight of a man in plain old clothes, his hand wrapped tightly around the inner door handle, his startled gaze darting around the room like a deer scanning for wolves. How did he get inside behind me without ringing the bell? Where the hell did he even come from?

"Welcome," I announce, attracting the man's attention.

"Welcome?" he parrots. His frightened eyes flick to me, a hollow stare as likely exhumed from the grave as dredged up from the depths of despair. He looks me up and down for a long moment, muttering incessantly, his pale fingers twitching spasmodically under the cuffs of his tattered coat before finally drifting away to continue scanning the room.

"Th—Thank you," he stutters, brushing a shaggy mane of brown hair back from his face and tugging on the collar of his coat. He drifts around me in a wide orbit, his knee-high boots clonking against the wood, their leather tops folded down and decorated with leaves on a vine. His clothes speak of a lustre long since lost, his eyes bloodshot. He has a ghostly white complexion in the soft candlelight. Thin like watered-down milk.

He passes me by, wandering towards the wall of weapons, and eying the assortment of blades with mild concentration. He lingers on a war-axe, then carries on, stepping up to the weapon studded wall and pulling the various swords down to swing them haphazardly before returning them to their rightful place.

"Need a hand with any of that?" I call after him, but he just fixes me with a haunted stare. He laughs abruptly, then turns to the table of trinkets and starts glossing over them, picking some up and frowning, then replacing them with others. I walk towards the counter, watching his animated movements with curiosity. Whatever he's searching for, it doesn't seem much like he is going to find it.

"Are you all right?" I ask, passing through the hatch and lowering it behind me before coming around to the counter proper. He jumps at the question, like he forgot I was there at all.

"What? Oh, yes. I'm fine," he says quickly, rushing across the floor towards the counter to meet me. "How are you? Are you alone?"

That old chestnut. Well, should he ask about any dogs, I'll do my best not to cleave his head from his shoulders.

"I am well," I reply, resting my arms on the bloodworm wood. "And yes, we are the only people here." Provided you don't consider doppelgängers to be a separate entity, I fail to mention.

He glances around like he can't quite believe what he's hearing.

"Ah, very good. Yes." The words tumble from his lips. He draws right up to the counter, his expression wild. "Listen. You've got to help me. He's coming. Could be here any minute. Gods, what did I do to deserve this? Mildred always scolded me for not going to church, but I never did listen. I'm an idiot, I tell you. A darn ruddy fool is what I am!"

"Slow down," I say, pumping the air with my palms while remaining calm for both of us. He seems a little mental. Acts a lot mental, too. Doesn't seem particularly dangerous though, so I'll entertain him. I've got plenty of supplies that can help remedy a simple case of assassination.

The man breathes a ragged sigh, casting a sweeping gaze around the room once more, like he expects someone is waiting to jump out at him. I eye the shadows of the room myself, though I am confident we are alone. In fact, I almost wish we weren't. Then maybe I would know where my assistant has gone off to. Turning back to my potential customer, I ask the obvious question.

"Is someone chasing you?"

"What?" he blurts, tensing harder than a neck caught in a noose. "Who said that? I mean, we're all running from something, aren't we? You and I aren't so different, you know?"

"I'm afraid I don't know."

The man just looks at me, like I'm talking crazy. Will irony never cease?

"No, no. Quite all right, my good man," he announces, like he's talking to someone else, only to lean uncomfortably close and whisper in a strained voice: "By all that is merciful, you've got to help me."

"How can I help?" I ask, feeling a little irritated and a lot confused.

"You never know when he's listening. Never know where he's hiding." He whips his head left and right, voice shrinking to a squeak while he draws his palm up to cover his lips. "Do you have more candles? He lurks in the shadows, you know."

"Who—"

"Shhh," the man snaps, shaking his head violently. "Mustn't say his name. Hear you, he will. Come running on the wind, quick as day turns to night."

Dread fills the man's features. The air of hopelessness that I've seen so many times is evident before me now. If experience is anything to go by, I know such fear cannot be faked so easily. Silently, I wondered if this was a distraction, but I decide to rule out a robbery. Besides, if someone were breaking into the back of my house right now, they would be knocked unconscious by a set of thunder scrolls rigged to clap. This guy's either lost his marbles, or is about to when his secret admirer shows up at the door. Frankly, neither is any of my concern. If he can't pay, he should sod off back to where he came from. But that's probably not what my assistant would do... Nor is it likely to land a sale. I need to change tactics. Build a customer relationship with this man, like my assistant did with the girl.

The man's stomach growls audibly, causing him to shake his head. He pulls a satchel around from behind him, one of a surprisingly old make, and unwinds the leather cord. He rummages through it for a moment, shaking his head again and prying free a few copper coins.

"Would you perchance have anything to eat that I could purchase? Only, I can't remember the last time I ate."

Observing his gaunt cheeks and the way the skin hung from his bones, I begrudgingly believe him. Perhaps this is my opportunity to build a rapport.

"Some bread and cheese, if it suits you. It isn't much, but if I'm being honest, I don't really deal in food."

He nods profusely, like a man dying of thirst staring at a pitcher of water. I guess he's not fussed.

"Wait there a moment," I say, my hand raised. "I'll fetch you something."

I move to the end of the counter where I keep my easy-access food, just in case the store gets busy. A little wishful thinking on my part, but humble beginnings and all that bollocks. Leaning down, I pull on a piece of cloth to uncover a loaf-end of hard bread and a block of cheese. I take up the bread knife and cut him a fat doorstop with a beautiful crust, then lever the blade through the block of cheese, severing it in two. Damn good cheese, that. Oh well. After wrapping the remaining food in the cloth, I decide to pour him a drink of water from the copper pitcher into a matching stein, too. I haven't met the man that can work through a piece of bread and cheese like this without a drink, but if I ever do, I'm sure it'll be in Hell. No mortal throat could ever hope to stand up to the task.

I pop up with the goods; the stein pinned to my side with my forearm, a plate in my hand like some old and crusty tavern wench. To my surprise, he's gone.

"The fuck?"

Surveying the shop, I spot his shaggy mane bobbing just above the table of scrolls. Using my free hand, I ease the hatch open and replace it down behind me, then walk around the table to his side. He's bent over an unfolded map, scratching his head and muttering to himself.

"Here you are." I place the plate on a bare patch of table, making him flinch.

"Oh. Oh, thank you, good sir."

He snatches the bread and cheese with desperate fingers and takes a large bite of both, chewing like a man who'd never tasted food in his miserable life. The dryness of the bread hits him and his eyes bulge. I hand him the drink of water. He nods eagerly like it was the only possible answer, and to my mind, that was certainly the case. He tips it back and drains the contents, gasping for breath as he swallows bread, cheese and water whole.

"Stupendous." He wipes his mouth on the back of his sleeve. "Simply wonderful. How much do I owe you?"

He retrieves the coppers from his pocket, frowns at them, then looks back up at me expectantly.

I stare down into his hand, the corner of my mouth tugging. "Ah, don't worry about it."

He opens his arms wide like a father greeting a long-lost son, squeezing my shoulders. "You are a man among men, good sir."

"Yeah, well... One good turn and all that." What the hell do I need with a few measly coppers, anyway? I need to make the big sale.

He beams at me, then turns his head back to the unfurled scroll pinned open to the table beneath a set of stone dragon paperweights. He waves his hand, then lets it drop mournfully to his side.

"I can make neither heads nor tails of this blasted thing. Is this where we are?"

I step closer and crane my neck around, spotting the chain running the border of the map. How anyone could not know that mark is beyond me. The Shattered Chain infested the world hundreds of years ago when they split from the parent order, the expansion of their dominion unrelenting in their self-righteous quest for the light. The map shows a series of towns pincered by mountain ranges along a deep valley, much like links in a chain. To the west of the valley and east of our current position, the jagged peaks of the Spinebreaker Mountains claw at the sky. Further to the east of the towns, the Dragontooth Spires stand sentinel like ancient towers atop the world.

"This is a map of the greater surrounding area," I say finally. "Are you looking for a local map?"

"Yes, I am. I need to keep heading west if I am to—" the words cut off in his throat as the candlelight flickers unsettlingly before us, puffing from existence, only to reignite anew. The hairs on the back of his neck visibly stand on end. "It matters not," he says quickly, wiping his brow and returning to the map.

I move the dragons, allowing the scroll to wind itself at the edges. A quick scan leads me to a map of the Shadowlands, the name given to the valleys wedged between the Spinebreaker foothills and the Everdark. Somewhat due to the vast amount of shade offered by the undulating hills, but mostly because the Everdark stands out like cancer on the skin of the world. I hold the new map up for him to see, pointing to the inked crest.

"This is where we are on any local maps you might see. Just keep an eye out for the chain snaking around the edges. That's how you know you're in Chain country."

My curious customer helps pull it open, sliding a dragon over old parchment into the corners of the map.

"This is where we are," I indicate, stabbing a finger at my lonely hill. "To the east is Glimmers' Reach. If you go west, you'll run into the Everdark forest." I shake my head. "Bad business for a man such as yourself to be going in there, especially in the dark. You won't live to see the other side."

He regards me sidelong, his lips pursed tight. They part as if to say something, though whether it is a confession or a plea for help, I cannot tell. Instead, he puffs up, a hint of resolve about him. Or perhaps misplaced bravado.

"It matters not," he sighs, tugging at his coat collar again. "I must continue west, come what may. I have not the luxury of options, and time is short."

"It's none of my business but... if you tell me what's after you, I can probably advise you on—"

"No," he snaps, making himself flinch. Years of horrors leaping from the festering shadows have left me unmoved to sudden outbursts, but make no mistake. You could cut the tension in here with a bloody knife. His lower lip quivers, and he immediately begins staring into the shadows of the room once more.

"I'm sorry," he whispers, turning back to me with a look of desperation. "How much for this?"

"It's worth two silver bits."

Our eyes meet, a silent conversation taking place

without words. I haven't got the money, he doesn't say. Too fucking bad, isn't my reply. But it bloody well should be. I'm running a business here, not a charity. Still... I know what it's like to be hunted without a hope or a prayer. No ally to rely upon, no way out in sight.

He reaches into his pocket, fishing out the coins and counting to himself, looking discouraged. Roughly seven pieces of copper to my eye, none of which I particularly recognise. It isn't nearly enough.

"Err, yes." His moustache twitches. "I seem to be, ah... This is rather embarrassing." He swallows hard, his gaze returning to the shadows before straightening his coat and his spine, his eyes hardening over. "You must forgive my impropriety. I will call upon your kindness no further, good sir. Thank you for your most generous hospitality, and for showing me the map."

Night Mother, help me, I'm being suckered by a fucking sob story. If he would stop being so damn polite, maybe I wouldn't have such a hard time kicking him out on his arse.

"Ah, just give me what you've got there." I growl, caving in like the pathetic, woodless, shivering-through-winter son of a bitch I really am.

His stony stare melts, moisture slick across his eyes. He bows low and takes my hand, placing the handful of copper coins into it and squeezing tight. "Thank you, sir. Thank you. Your kindness shall not be forgotten."

Bastard's trying to make me blush. Something moves past the side window, and I snap to it, spotting my missing assistant walking on by.

"What's that?" the customer cries, whirling around to see what I was looking at, but my assistant has already vanished.

"Nothing," I lie. "Just thought I saw some distant lightning on the horizon."

I clear my throat, turning my attention back to the map.

"See this road?" I ask the man, pointing to a winding black line in a bid to bring him back around. "It leads around the edge of the Everdark. Stay on it and you'll get to the other side, and you might even do it without being eaten alive or strung up by bandits."

"Hmm. Yes, I see. Thank you so much," he says again, nodding his way along the thick black line. Satisfied, he takes off his satchel and places it on the table with a heavy thud, then removes the stone dragon and rolls up the map, when an unexpected chill blusters through the room, snuffing out candles for good this time, deepening the growing shadows to pitch.

My customer jolts, shunting the table and nearly falling to the floor, what little colour remaining in his face draining away like a leaky bucket.

The air becomes cold and heavy, and I can see my breath billowing out in front of me. Dark whispers fill the emporium, a disturbing sound that has me reaching for my silver.

Something catches in my peripheral, twisting me around to see a shroud of shadow skulking along the far wall, swimming silently over the luminous potions like a shark beneath the waves. It eats the light of everything it touches, the potions winking out like stars in a morning sky, only to be reborn in the shadow's wake. Following the trail, I realise something drags in its hand. A thin pole with a wicked curved blade that cleaves the potions' light anew. What the fuck has this guy been doing? This is no normal monster tailing him, of that, I am sure.

We watch the shadow circle the rest of the room, sliding

onto the floor and under the door, out of sight. Quelled light blooms in its absence, and suddenly the air is free of that cold, oppressive weight. What in the world was that thing?

"God help me, he's coming," my condemned guest blurts, snatching up the map and rushing past me towards the wall of potions. "Hide yourself if you value your life, friend. Our kind are not long for this world!"

"What is it?" I ask, still gripping the dagger handle tucked into my waistline and scanning around the room. "What's chasing you?"

No longer sensing a disturbance, I flick back to my customer by the potion wall. But he's gone. I stand there, blinking, looking around the shop floor once more. What? Where the hell did he go?

More confused than ever, I ease around the table to check the floor, crouching down painfully low to see beneath the tables. Nothing. He's gone. He's actually gone.

"What in the world is going on here?"

I scratch my forehead with my knuckle, staring down at the fistful of copper coins. Each one is stamped inaccurately with the emblem of a bearded king beneath a strange, pointed tower. I don't recognise them, but they appear to be ancient. Upon closer inspection, the copper looks impure, and probably isn't worth a damn. On the other hand, if these are real, they're probably worth a great sum to a collector. Or maybe a historian.

I survey the shop once more and even do a lap around the building, inside and out. While rubbing my arms against the bracing wind, I keep an eye out for my wayward assistant every step of the way. I test the creak of the front door and the tinkle of the bell on the way past—twice— until I'm standing back where I started beside the table of scrolls, stumped as a coppiced tree.

"Some night," I mutter, picking up one of the coins and turning it over in my hand. "Not sure if I got robbed, or I did the robbing."

I glance over the scattering of scrolls, thinking to wind up that map of the Chain when I spot the missing customer's satchel resting open on the table. I step forward, my foot squishing through something soft and slick.

"Ugh... what the hell?" Lifting my boot from the slop, it reveals a small pile of chewed-up bread and cheese, doused in a puddle of water.

"What? Where did this come from?" My mind races. The man had been standing here beside the table when he consumed the food and drink. He'd eaten every crumb. I watched him polish it off in a few bites, yet here the food lies all over my new damn floor. Judging from the size of the pile, it's every sodding bit of it.

I rub the back of my neck, feeling a sudden chill returning to the air. The room feels unsafe, the dark spaces threatening, but nothing stares back. On edge, I turn to the abandoned satchel laid open on the table.

"Hmph... in such a rush, he left it behind." I reach out to take it, then hesitate, superstitions rousing. "Oh, grow up, you big girl."

I snatch the bag from the table and sling it over my shoulder. I'll just put it behind the counter in case he comes back. It's unusually heavy, but I don't want to pry. Wood creaks around me, the house yawning against the moaning overhead wind whistling outside. It's always windy on the hill, I remind myself. There's no tree cover.

Now that I'm alone, I notice just how dark it is in here with the candles snuffed out. Usually, the dark is my friend, but I would be lying if that strange man's warnings hadn't put my hackles up. Scared isn't the right word for it. I haven't felt real fear since I was a pup. But a man would have to be crazy to not take heed of the unknown.

Forcing my shoulders to relax, I hurry across the room to the nearest lit candle and pick up a long, thin wooden splint, burning the end until it takes a flame. It doesn't take me long to whiz around the shop and light every damn wick, torch, and fireplace in the house, despite my near dry stash of remaining wood.

A healthy blaze rests in my hip too, the one fire I could honestly do without. Suppose it's better to burn in the leg than rot in the ground. And speaking of burn, where the hell's that whisky at? I light the last of the candles, satisfied with the warm glow running through my shop. Now, if something were to come knocking through the shadows, it would find itself face to face with a wall of burning light. And me standing behind it, with enough silver to make the Pope's fat arse reel in his gilded chair.

"Right. Got to log the disappointing sale, then it's time for that stiff drink." My mind wanders back to that shadow demon gliding along the walls, or whatever the hell it was. Glancing over my shoulder for any lingering pockets of darkness, I decide to hurry up and make that drink before anything else can go wrong on this crazy night.

CHAPTER SIX

Split rounds crackle and snap in the hearth, the deathly thin supply of oak burning slow and steady, washing my bedchamber in soft orange light. It's not dreadfully cold inside, but you never can be too careful. Not all visitors travel across the physical planes of this world. Many prefer to walk along strange passageways unseen by the eyes of men. And besides, something about what that crazy bastard said didn't sound so crazy after all. Perhaps I'm just tired, but I don't think it so. The night is and always has been my domain. It's probably nothing, though I can't shake the feeling there is a kernel of truth about his words. About the hunter nipping at his heels from the shadows. Where there's smoke, there's fire, so the old saying goes.

The first of night's rain patters on the windowpane, prompting me to lean forward at my desk and gaze up into the silver moonlit sky, a frown etching across my face. Not a cloud in sight.

I lean a little further, my old chair squeaking beneath me. The edge of dark rolling clouds peek into view, smothering the studded starlight in a thick haze. The stench of ozone lingers on the breeze seeping through the window crack. A storm is brewing. I lean all the way and pull the window closed when the drizzle takes hold, a promise of worse to come. Wouldn't want to snuff out my reading light. Nor do I have a need for puddles. The heated floor would burn them away before long, but I'll ward against them all the same.

The roll of parchment the strange man was carrying in his satchel lies restrained across my desk, the ends fighting to curl back and protect its secrets from prying eyes. That's okay. They don't help ease my concern, anyway. Nothing but a bunch of babbling about dead men walking the Earth. As if anyone needs to hear that crap, what with all the nightmares crawling around out there as it is. Leave the dead in the ground where they belong. Bah, what good can reading this garbage really do me?

Shadows flicker along the old wooden desk, dancing beneath the sway of guttering candles. I tighten the scroll and stuff it back into the crazy man's satchel, clearing a space for an old tome that takes up most of the bag. Despite him carrying it on his person, dust and cobwebs stick to the book like a second skin.

I drum my fingers on the desk, distracted. A quick glance over my shoulder assures me that all is well, for now. Just my imagination playing tricks on me. Another glance, but at the mirror resting to one side, reveals my assistant to be on the shop floor, busying himself with cobwebs of his own. Good enough, though I would like to have a word with him at some point. To see what he's been up to. Every time I try to get a bead on him, the busybody is either somewhere I cannot discern for looking, or taking a long piss off a tall cliff. There's a perfectly good outhouse out back, but I would run the risk of being labelled a hypocrite if I said anything to that effect.

Instead, I drag the dusty tome closer, its leather binding brushing over the wood with a hiss. I wipe my palm over the cover and give it a blow, trying not to sneeze my brains across the desk when a cloud of dust plumes around my head. Coughing and spluttering, I wave at the air. Should've kept that damn window open. The cover depicts several symbols. One I recognise startles me. A shattered blade sits at the centre of the tome, a chain spiralling around it.

"The Shattered Blade of Ruin."

For this tome to bear the old mark, it must be ancient. It's been well over a thousand years since the Blade split from the Chain, becoming the fractured orders of today.

My jaw sets tight. I fish a medallion from beneath my clothes and stare at the symbol adorning the disc of solid silver that hangs around my neck. The shattered sword it bears is unchained, worn from years of wear. The heavy metal is warmed by the fires beneath my ribs, the flames fanned through a lifetime of war. The symbol of my order, or what's left of it, anyway. A dying breed of men. There's probably none of us left. It still has the three claw marks cutting diagonally through the centre. I never did get around to fixing it. Never saw the need. Now, well... I let it fall from my touch; the silver clinking heavily against my chest. I reach out to open the tome's cover but snatch my fingers back when I spot the tremor in my hand. Why am I shaking? Staring at my weathered skin and the telltale marks of another life, I clench my fist, forcing the shudder to dissipate.

"Hmph..." Just the jitters of an old man, I reassure myself.

The pages peel back, yellowed and cracked, written in

the hard script of the old world. It's been years since I've read anything penned by their hand. Decades, even. Not since my fellow Blade, Cormack, had brought word of our master's death. So many years ago, now. It feels like I'm recalling another man's life in the vaguest of detail.

Outside, the rain gives way to a deluge, giving the cosy room a cave-like feel. Wonder how that weirdo is faring, skulking along the Everdark alone in the pouring rain? I've had some strange encounters, but that one was right up there. Perhaps I can glean something from his effects, after all. Squinting at the pages, my mind flares with the ache of remembering. The script begins to shift before my very eyes, revealing the hidden meaning. It's not code, but such time has passed since it was written that it could easily be mistaken for it. Language, much like life, is in a constant flux of change. Now is no different.

"Brennan Ruin," I whisper, brushing my old fingers over the worn pages. "God's king, and founder of the Chained Blades of Ruin. Champions of light sworn to stand vigilant against the dark, their holy mission—Bah."

I shove it away, not sure if I'm reading a history lesson or some moron's idea of one. It's not wrong, of course, but the notion of light and dark, of good and evil? Such ideals have long since abandoned me, leaving naught but a grey, bitter taste in my mouth. To call the Blades warriors of light is laughable; and the Chain even more so. Good men fled to the darkness, where we stood a fighting bloody chance, while the Chain lorded their so-called piety in the light of day, more interested in bringing their fellow man to heel than that which harrows them.

I once thought such men were corrupt. Lost from the path that they had set out on long ago. Now, I know different. It is not corruption, nor misguidance that leads them astray. It is merely the way of the world, and the final destination of all things. Suffering is the only guarantee in this life; and if you're lucky, an early grave. And it makes me wonder if such words had been written by the young; bright-eyed and inexperienced in the ways of the world. Or maybe their conviction was greater than my own. I, too, once held the Order in high esteem when I was little more than a pup. Back when I thought I could make a difference. No longer.

"Hmph." I push the damn tome aside and fold my arms. I've got better things to do than read this crap, like stave off the sodding chill. I rub my palms together. No one ever mentioned how goddamn cold you get in your golden years. Nor what's so bloody golden about them, neither. All these happy thoughts make me need a fucking drink.

Sliding the chair back with a screech, I rise on achy bones and drift across the room towards the fireplace, staring into its flickering depths for the demons that haunt it. My demons, I recall, and ever by my side. I slide between the leather chairs and the small table that separates them, my toes digging into the soft brown bear fur beneath my feet. A gift from Marston many name-days gone, being the old crack-shot hunter that he is. He's not one for bothering the bears, but this one had become a little too partial to human flesh, and had traded the quiet of woodland berries for attacking convoys travelling along the road. Big bastard, too, in comparison to other bears. Snuffles was his name, as far as the kids were concerned.

It wasn't until Marston put one in its eye from a hundred paces with his crossbow that the carnage ceased. That's what Marston said at least. Given his aim, it wouldn't surprise me if he made that shot from a damn sight further. I still need to get the old goat something of equal worth from my collection. Only, the more I search, the more I come to realise not burdening him with any of this crap is the real gift. Let the bastard live in peace.

Just the thought of fighting something like this exhausts me, and I fall into my chair, the old leather soft and cracked from years of suffering my arse. At this point, it's by far the more worn of the pair, but I could never bring myself to sit in its companion. That was my wife's favourite chair, and I refuse to let anyone sully her memory. Perhaps that's a little crazy, hoping against hope to find her sitting there again one day, a paintbrush in her hand and a curse on her lips, lashing her latest creation with barbed love until it damn near leaps off the canvas. Night Mother, I miss her. More now than ever. My head sinks to the tune of my mood, and I find myself longing for that sweet amber relief I've been saving all year. Hits like a fireball to the face and burns twice as hard, a bit like the missus. Can't knock it, unless it's back, that is. I turn to the side table, reaching for the bottle and take hold of thin air.

"The hell?" I snap around to gaze upon the lonely pair of glasses on the polished table. The bottle is nowhere to be seen. In my surprise, I feel the onset of a heart attack, but I decide to call it off until I've checked the under-shelf. Leaning forward in my chair, I double over with a curse of my own and crane my neck to investigate the small cavity where sweet relief sleeps.

"Gone!"

My chest spasms with pain, eager to get things rolling. I would like to roll some heads, were there any within reach to do so. Clutching my ribs, I fall to my knees onto Snuffles' forgiving fur, collapsing in a heap of self-pity; more to check under the chairs than anything else. Beneath those hard, sculpted wooden legs, only devastation awaits. And a needle and thread beneath Sil's chair that makes my heart ache for real. Damn it all. No pipe. No whisky. No woman. This is the pits. There's got to be something around here for me to get my fix. Desperate times call for desperate measures, so I disregard the glass and pull out the pitcher. Should I find anything substantial, I'm going to need the upgrade.

With my heart attack getting me nowhere, I begrudgingly climb to my feet and saunter over to the cupboards lining the wall, where I keep odds and ends that might be useful, out of sight. It wouldn't be the first time I've neglected a stacked bottle of the good stuff in the shadows, only to happen upon the bugger when I've needed it most. I cross my fingers, praying to whatever god happens to be on duty for a goddamn miracle, and yank open the door.

Spiderwebs and old twine greet me, and I respond by slamming the door in their fucking face.

"Bollocks it all to Hell! And why is it so cold in here?" And why didn't my bastarding hip get the message? Son of a bitch is burning hotter than syphilis... or so I hear.

Irritated to breaking point, I grab my knobbled wooden cane leaning against the chair's arm for some sweet relief and ease across the room, making my way to the hook hanging on the wall by the door. I grab the dark leather jerkin hanging from its end, sliding my arms through the holes, one at a time. The leather should help keep me plenty warm, and it's pretty good for keeping a few extra blades out of sight, too. I slip it over my fresh white linen tunic, leaving the sleeves long and loose.

Old hands brush against older leather, my calloused fingers catching on the blood red stitching over the left breast, the large B and the initial thread of an 'A' breaking the smooth surface. I follow the stitch with my index finger, old memories weighing heavy on my heart. Sil was stitching this for me before she... hmph. Said she liked the idea of me playing shopkeeper, but then she always was a kinky one. Never thought it would actually happen. Funny, the turns life takes.

And speaking of funny turns. I fetch the mirror from my bedside table, hoping my assistant isn't still pissing in the wind. To my surprise, he's in the stockroom sorting through inventory, his presence perhaps masked by the now cacophonous storm. The balls on that bastard. Must take after me. The view of parchment and quill slides across the round table, sighting the—I gasp, shock and horror bleaching my bones to the marrow.

"The fuck?" I bellow, pressing my nose against the mirror so hard it's a wonder neither breaks. "That's my whisky!"

The traitorous alcoholic pours himself a tidy measure, lifting it silently to his lips and knocking it back like it's bloody free.

"Oh, hell no." I throw the mirror on to the bed and rush for the hallway door, my cane slamming the wood with justified rage. There's no way he's polishing that whole damn bottle off by himself without me. No way in—

As I storm past the shop floor, the front door bursts open, bell jingling with panic, the fire's light across the room fluttering with fear. Cold wind seeps to infect the warmth of my shop, blustering past the insidious silhouette stalking my doorway that slams me to a stop and cranes my neck.

Across the room, a cloak of the blackest night rolls ominously at the silhouette's back. Their eyes burn blood red in the night, freezing me in place and chilling the blood in my veins. Is that him, I wonder? The one who hunts? I can't help but swallow, my hand caressing the blade nestled in the small of my back. I look back down the hall to the stockroom door, hatred and fire simmering in my throat. But I've got no choice. If I'm going to beat that bastard at his own game and prove my worth, then it's now or never. Steeling my nerve, I step behind the counter, ready to serve.

Win or lose, I've got a job to do.

CHAPTER SEVEN

The front room of my store feels exposed to the elements. Storm-winds swirl cold amongst the rafters above my head. Only when I step out from behind the relative safety of my bloodworm counter does the drop in temperature become truly apparent. A bastion of warmth and shelter only moments ago. The shop now feels like a cold sink at the bottom of the hill, a deathly chill lingering over an open grave. Another breath of wind howls through the front door, snagging the shadow's cloak and snuffing out more candles across the shop floor, each one succumbing to my visitor's will.

"Welco—" I attempt to say, but the greeting trails off when I glimpse what has skulked in from the night, or rather, that which I cannot see.

The door is peeled back and caught in the wind. Within the frame stands an absence shrouded in night, obscured by the sideways rain hammering at their back. Pale, boney fingers breach the shadows. They grip the door frame, their talon-like fingernails raking the scorchwood, as though trying to prevent themselves from being sucked into the abyss beyond. Or perhaps they are trying to keep from being repelled.

"Welcome." I growl, flexing my wrists instinctively, loosening off my blade arm. The air of the shop smells different somehow. Death's smog leeches across it, creeping like a poisonous mist to sour my nostrils. "Won't you come inside?"

"Yes..." whispers a voice, distant, yet eerily close to my ear, those ravenous eyes almost lost within an impenetrable cowl. They burn with blood-soaked light in the absence of candle flame. Wet, bulging, and brimming with desire. This customer has a need, though whether that concerns buying my wares or gracing the shop floor with their corpse has yet to be determined. I place my cane to one side. Of all the protection at my disposal, a length of old wood probably ranks pretty damn low on the scale.

"I need..." the figure whispers, almost reading my thoughts. He slides into the shop like a shade, clinging to the dark spaces between the candelabra. His footsteps make no noise, his movements laboured, yet predatory. Even without light, those eyes sparkle with hunger, a primordial instinct that kicks my fight-or-flight responses into action; and I never choose the latter. That distinct twinge in my gut. The needling of nerves down my spine. There's no mistaking this one. A bloodsucker stains my floor.

I fold my arms, trying to restrain my eager fingers so ready to grace my blade. It's probably not enough, but it's nice to have options. And speaking of options, that's why I keep the arm's length of silver beneath my countertop. For special occasions, because sometimes a knife just won't cut it. That sword has seen me through decades of blood and guts, of horror and heresy. The fouler the beast, the deeper it cuts, and the wounds never close. Now might be as good a time as any to unleash the real arsenal, but this might be a genuine customer I'm dealing with; and to my knowledge, there's no faster way to piss off a bloodsucker than drawing a silver sword on the unsuspecting son of a bitch.

Instead, I show a measure of decorum and slide the blade sheathed uncomfortably in my arse crack, placing it on the desk between us on my guest's approach. That halts his advance. Makes him think twice about trying to bleed a dodgy old man. He lingers on the knife for a long while, his head sinking between hunched shoulders.

"If you want blood, you'll have to buy it, friend," I say plainly, appealing to the humanity within him. Just on the off chance that there's a shred of it left. No need to play games with this one. I've carved my way through enough of his tainted brethren in my time to know with what I'm dealing. Much like humans, the degree of a vampire's power varies, but they all smell the same. Most are little more than rabid dogs hunting in packs. These days, people call them ravagers. This one appears to be alone, and much further along in his evolution. The oldest blood amongst the vampire hordes boasts horrific power and speed, with minds sharp enough to outwit the craftiest of hunters. Long in the tooth, deep in the vein, so Master Abraham used to say.

"Blood..." slithers the whisper of a word, serpentine on my customer's tongue. Lapping sounds emanate from his jaw like he can taste it just thinking about it. He doesn't look away from the knife. Stares at it with unbreakable intrigue.

"No, not now," he says, finally. "I am in need of..." his words tail off into the darkness, his eyes burning red like stars. They pulse rhythmically, while his animated posture, frozen. Hairs stand on end along my arms when I make the connection. He isn't staring at the knife. He's peering beneath the skin to the artery in my wrist.

The muscles in my back tighten as I realise what is happening. His eyes. They're pulsing to the beat of my heart.

I snap my fingers, breaking his trance, the star-fire ebbing from his gaze. He looks at me with surprise from those unsearchable depths, though I still cannot glean his face.

"You are not like the others," the man whispers, drawing pale hands together and interlocking wicked black nails over his stomach. "Why, you are almost as cold as I."

Can't argue with that. In any other moment of my life, I would've vaulted the counter and punched silver through the bastard's shrivelled heart... but doing so won't pay the bills, and the night dwellers have an uncanny ability to sniff out killing grounds where others of their kind have fallen. I would be cutting the legs out from under my business before it even got off the ground.

"So, what do you need? Or did you just come to window shop my veins?"

The vampire hunches up again, as if unsure how to proceed. I hear his tongue rubbing against his dry lips within the depths of that black cowl.

"I had a run-in, of sorts," he says, carefully.

"Can you be more specific?"

With a hiss, the vampire reaches into his cloak, prising something free. Beneath it, I catch sight of a fine black coat marbled dark crimson and buttoned in gold. He dumps a cloth parcel on the table like it was freshly pulled from a blacksmith's forge.

"Go ahead," he offers, gesturing towards the parcel. "It will not bite again."

I slide my knife under the fold and flick the fabric open. The revelation makes my eyebrows reach for the rafters. The vampire—or rather, my customer—shudders at the sight of the silver bolt resting on the cloth. Its jagged teeth are covered in coagulated blood, the back end in what could be charred wisps of skin. The bolt is fashioned into a tri-point head, the mark of my brothers. The shape of the bolt keeps the wound from closing. Such a technique doesn't make so much difference for a vampire. Over time, they'll succumb to silver poisoning, regardless of the wound; but there are many other things averse to silver in the wilds for which such crude measures can make all the difference.

In the recesses of my mind, I wonder if my brethren are near. Might be tracking him at this very moment. Could arrive at my door. What would I say to them if they did? Would they even recognise me? Here, of all places, selling services to the creatures we swore to destroy. A younger zealot would name me tainted by the darkness, and honestly, I might not have the stomach to deny such truths.

I drum my fingers together, weighing the odds of being massacred either by this guest or the next. Well… This customer's here right now, and he looks to have coin, so consider my loyalty won. Ready to deal, I point my blade tip at the vampire's stomach.

"Show me."

Warily, he pulls back the folds of his cowl, revealing the pale white of his face, the blood-red of his eyes. He looks waxy. Dead. More than they usually do, at any rate. He doesn't have a single hair on his head, the smooth skin of his skull riddled with veins of frozen blue and black lightning. For reasons that elude me, I thought he would have hair.

The vampire grimaces. He parts the luxurious cloak and unbuttons his coat, revealing a once expensive grey tunic now stained dark red. Beneath, a gruesome, bloody puncture rests above his hip, the grey skin scorched black and crisp around the edges. A thick, black blob of something leaks from the wound, making him suck air through sharp teeth. The smell of soured blood curdles my nose, though I can't tell if it's coming from the wound or his mouth.

"It burns," he hisses through clenched teeth.

"I bet it does. Tell me, where did this happen?"

"Beyond the Spinebreaker Pass. Nowhere near here."

I nod slowly. There is still every chance a Blade would track him here. None give up the hunt so easily. I sigh.

"You've travelled far, especially for someone wounded. I can treat it, but you'll have to come around back." I glance at the hallway door behind me, my jaw tightening at the thought of my assistant standing over an empty bottle, and a fiend of the fires who cannot abide my presence. I can't help but swallow. "That's where I keep my medical supplies."

The vampire looks at me quizzically. "And you believe such techniques will work on a..." He rolls his hand, searching for the right word. "... on someone like me?"

"Not the usual kind, no," I admit, turning back to my new patient. "But this isn't the usual kind of shop."

"Indeed," he says, glancing around as if for the first time. He lingers on the weapons adorning the walls before settling back on me, seemingly stuck between two minds. "Very well."

He releases the folds of his tunic, offering a hand. "Lead on."

I move towards the counter partition and place my hand beneath the wood, fighting a grimace without my abandoned cane. Should really use the bastard thing, but this is no time to appear weak.

"No. After you," I insist, raising the partition.

He stares at me warily. Suddenly, our roles have reversed. I'm no longer the prey in his eyes. Little does he know, I never was.

"Through here?" the vampire asks, sliding across the veil and drifting towards the doorless frame of the rear hallway. Gingerly, he glances around the corner, like he expects an axe to guillotine through his neck. I resist the urge to smile.

"Turn left and down the hall. Go through the door. Sit at the table."

He does my bidding, though, remaining side-on where he can keep me in his sights. He steps carefully into my supply room, his hand lingering on the door, with me following a short distance behind. The small hearth burns gently to one side, the embers low and suffering from neglect. It isn't the most comfortable room in the house, but it's warm enough. Though I doubt he really cares.

To my surprise, my assistant is nowhere to be seen. Again. The bottle is gone from the table along with him, the messy piles on the table now organised into some kind of system I've yet to make sense of. Were I the one doing it, I would've separated scrolls by magic and knowledge, and physical items into varying categories of most likely to unleash all hell.

"Forgive the mess," I say quickly, guiding him towards an empty chair by the table. "I'm still organising."

"Quite the collection you have," he notes, lingering on a bronze bauble resting on the table while he takes a slow seat.

"I've been around." Staring at the piles of items, I see my assistant has organised it exactly to my standard. Guess I can't be mad about that, but there's still plenty else to go around. "If you'll bear with me, I've just got to locate my tools."

"By all means."

I step up to a pile of wooden crates and break open the first, my breath catching when I glean what awaits inside. Neatly folded dresses, wild with colour. I run my finger over the silky-smooth fabric of a yellow dress with white polka dots. Beside it, a luxurious piece of dark satin shimmers like ink in the steady glow of nearby candlelight. I lift it out of the box and hold it to my cheek. Smokey and dangerous... it still smells of her, too. I stifle a sigh and put back the folded dress, carefully replacing the lid. Trust her, even now, to fight for my attentions.

With a grunt, I shift the crate from the top to reveal the next waiting beneath and crack it open. Inside, I spot what I'm looking for. A couple of vials filled with murky water. Sourced from the Everdark swamp, where the Dread Mother poisons her waters with leeching roots. A paralytic toxin for anything organic. It seeps through the skin and sees its victims falling beneath the dark waters where she can break them down and nourish her forest.

Having lived near the swamp for much of my life, I've developed somewhat of an immunity. Enough that a few splashes won't bother me, anyway. The poison serves as a peculiarly effective remedy for cursed flesh; not that I'm about to tell him that. Fortunately for humanity, the denizens of the dark are rather lacking in the medicinal fields. A blind spot brought about by their unnatural resilience and healing abilities; but that game plan goes right down the shitter when it comes to a bolt of silver.

"Just you here tonight?" the vampire asks, a dangerous air to an otherwise harmless question. "Or perhaps... you live alone."

I can't tell if he's up to something, but I can definitely say an extra pair of hands wouldn't waylay him in the event of a throw-down, so I decide to stick with the truth. Honesty is always the best policy, right up until it isn't, then you lie like you just took a shit on your own mother's Sunday best and pray to whoever the fuck's listening that your arse cheeks survive the backhand.

"It's just me." Technically, that's true, but the whole truth could take some explaining, and I'm in no mood for such conversations. Turning my mind from that particular shitstorm, I reach for a pair of sharp shears and some bandages before grabbing a candle and moving to the ebbing heat of the fire, holding the wick to one of the glowing embers. A flame blooms into life on the candle's end, flaring and then shrinking again, as though shying away.

Easing up, I pause. The crazy demon bitch's stone vase swirls magenta atop the mantel before me until it burns almost hot pink, stealing my fortitude. It looks as though the patina was never there, the solid shape now clear like thin glass beneath the magically infused chains criss-crossing its body. A fiery script forms on the vase's surface, motes of flame flicking from the letters like exploding stars while it scrawls out a clipped, curt message, making my brow furrow. It reads...

"Stupid old bastard."

A knot tightens in my chest as the message fades away. A glassy sunrise turned to cold grey stone once more, leaving me empty. Summoning the will to carry on, I turn around, pressure blooming against my skin like I've walked into an invisible wall. I'm standing face to face with the vampire. Sweat beads his forehead, his red eyes wide and dilated. I didn't even hear the son of a bitch move.

"That wound will never heal," I say coolly, resorting to a lifetime of experience in a bid to wrest control of my pulse. A pumping heart is no better than waving your tasty arse at a ravenous chimaera. The beast can't help but hunt you down and tear you limb from limb in a blood-soaked craze. Play my cards wrong and this'll likely go no differently. "Take a seat."

The vampire rapidly blinks, yanking himself from the call to hunt.

"Yes," he says, shaking the craze away and drawing a handkerchief to dab at his sweat speckled forehead. "Yes... Forgive me."

He turns away, his languishing body scarcely carrying him back to the table. He collapses into the seat and runs his boney fingers over his skull, making him appear haggard and old. And maybe he is. Could be a thousand years old for all I know. Poor bastard. Who the hell would want that?

With my guest in his seat, I glance at the bundle of scrolls gathered at the corner of the table. Memories stir. They are a collection I relieved from a crackpot wizard in a dark, stone tower, if one could ever believe it. The golden silk that binds them together is riddled with faded amber words of magic that glimmer against the dark. I cannot decipher them all, but there is a faded portion that I can make out that reads: "Break—Scrolls."

Ah, yes. I remember now. The breaker scrolls. Fonts of untold destruction that could sunder the world with but a flick of the page. Legends have been told about them. That the spells inked within can level mountains and shatter city walls like glass cast against the rocks. Their power is not to be underestimated, and only the greatest of practitioners could ever hope to harness vibrations so well as to not break themselves along the way. I should probably put them somewhere a little more secure, but for now, I have other business to attend.

I move to my guest's side and place the instruments on the table beside him, catching his tired gaze.

"Before I do this, I need to know you can afford to pay for the treatment."

"Hmm? Oh, yes, yes." Irritated, he waves his hand, the other still dabbing his cheeks, until he reaches into his pocket and roots around. Eyes widening, he tries his other pocket, his fingers slowing upon realisation. One that's going to leave me a little light on payment, if I'm not mistaken. He rises from his seat, his thoughts swimming behind those deathly glowing eyes. "I appear to find myself in a bit of a quandary..."

Though he rises with dignity, I can see the smack of embarrassment on his face. A quandary indeed. If I were him, I would be thinking about how much face I could save by killing the son of a bitch I can't afford to pay. Maybe drain him dry too, pad out the damage a little, see if I can't push through the pain and come out the other side. Just like all those other times, where I rolled the dice and beat the odds. Every mother fucker thinks he's the main character in this shitty life. Can do what they want and get away with it, too.

He looks at me, and I can't help but do the same. The tightness of his lips. The spasmodic twitch of his veins. The bastard's thinking about it. Before thoughts can turn to teeth, I pre-emptively open my own maw of destruction.

"It's on the house," I blurt, the blow of such a statement nearly bringing me to my knees.

"On... the house?" the vampire asks, caught off-guard, craning his head slightly. "I see. A new customer incentive, I suppose." He smiles, regaining his composure.

"Right..." I hold out my hand, fighting the urge to make a fist. "Take a seat."

Somewhat disarmed, the vampire returns to his chair.

This might be costing me a sale, but it's undoubtably buying me years. Maybe that's wishful thinking so late in the day, but at this point I would call even half-right a win. The air feels a little less unsettled, and I begrudgingly ease down onto a knee beside the table to do my work when the vampire's body tenses, his attention snapping to the door, his eyes pulsing blood red.

"I thought you said it was just you."

I crane my own neck around to see the hallway door swing wide. We both leap to standing. My assistant slides through the door with a pilfered bottle in one hand and a piece of parchment in the other, a tuneless noise spilling from his blasphemous lips. He lifts the bottle to eye-height and smiles like a thieving bastard, grinning like an idiot hogging all the sauce.

"Yooou make me piss like a bleedin' wizard." He laughs, cocking an eye at the bottle. He takes another ungodly swig, making me convulse with quiet rage, only to look our way and freeze on the spot. Once distant thunder now rolls overhead, a backdrop of slanted light painting the fire-lit scene black and white. Dressed in the same loose linen and my spare jerkin, that bastard is my perfect twin.

"Ah..." my double says, glancing back and forth between me and the vampire, then scratches his head with the parchment. "Shit."

CHAPTER EIGHT

BENEATH THE HAMMERING DELUGE, silence reigns. Bars of white light flash between the slats of drawn shuttered windows, slicing the shadows at my feet across the stockroom floor, and melding with hearth's light. Across the floorboards, my doppelgänger licks his sugar-dried lips, all the while clutching the gorgeous bottle of smoke-barrel whiskey in his bastard hands. How the hell am I supposed to explain this to my customer?

"Ah, mhm," my double growls, acknowledging our presence. "I'll just err... Mhm." He nods with great conviction, turning unsteadily away and pulling the door closed behind him, leaving us in the awkward sober silence.

I feel my customer's red-hot stare lingering on me.

"And I suppose that is your twin brother, yes?" The vampire flicks his cloak out behind him and retakes his seat, his steady gaze unwavering.

"Sure. Why not?" I take a knee and arrange my tools, consisting of a pair of small shears, some clean bandage cloth and a vial, on the edge of the table, and breathe out a long slow breath. Fuck if I can be bothered to argue the toss.

It can be whatever he wants it to be. I'm a dodgy old man offering illegal services to denizens of the night, not some fairy-fucking-godmother dishing out wishes like blowjobs on payday. Goddamn, I need a drink.

"Oh," my customer says, reaching beneath his cloak and pulling out a small silk bag. "I forgot about this."

He opens the bag and retrieves a few coins from within, placing them into my hand.

"A tip. For seeing me so urgently. I confess I do not know if they are worth anything. It has been so long since I walked in such circles. I deal in a different form of currency these days." His eyes flash with those last words, and I decide not to request clarity. Staring down at the coins, I realise he has given me four copper pieces. Basically worthless. It makes me smile.

The vampire nods. "You are satisfied. Are you not?"

His words smack of aristocratic arrogance, but he seems to truly desire me content. Amusing, if nothing else.

"Most satisfied," I assure him, and he sits back, relieved. I flip the coins over in my palm, revealing a cross wreathed in chain on each, the stamp marks slightly off-centre.

"I see you've spent time along the Chain," I mutter, pocketing the coins and leaning in to address his wound. "Dangerous territory for your kind."

He shoots me a look, his posture shifting between tense and relaxed.

"Yes, well... To feed, one goes where one must," he says, reluctantly drawing his tunic apart, the charred hole in his stomach emitting a fetid smell into the room. "The greater the danger, the greater the livestock. Now so more than ever."

"Makes sense. Sit to the side, legs behind the table leg and hands on the tabletop."

He does as I bid him. With only a gentle prod, the vampire's lips tighten into a sneer, revealing vicious fangs. He eyes the instruments in my hand, and to my surprise, complies.

I lean down and uncover the wound, making him hiss again. "This is going to hurt. I must cut away the burnt skin."

"But—"

"It will spread."

A long silence. Makes my damn hip ache like a son of a bitch.

"Very well," he replies.

I begin my work, cutting carefully at the burnt, extra-dead skin. Silver on the dead acts like gangrene on the living. If you don't cut it off, you'll die of blood infection or poisoning before long. Or re-die, I suppose. Would that make him redead, or un-undead? Personally, I wish the fuckers would just get it right the first time. Would've made my job a shit ton simpler over the years, but then I probably shouldn't complain. If that were the case, I wouldn't be here either.

My patient hisses with every snip but keeps his arms and legs where I told him to. It isn't exactly safe, but as long as he needs me to do my work, I should be fine. Just a different kind of danger that comes with a different kind of job. No worse than hunting the bastards down and cleaving their heads from their shoulders in the depths of ruined castles and the homes of terrified villagers. So who really cares?

"So," the vampire says between winces, "does this place have a name?"

"Hmph... The Emporium of Many Things, I suppose."

"Accurate," he concedes, "though a little vague. And you? Do you have a name? I see the letter B stitched on to your clothes."

I continue cutting, trying not to follow the vampire's gaze. "Purveyor," I reply. "The jerkin belonged to an old friend. I just never removed the stitches."

The vampire smiles. "I see."

"You?"

He pauses at that, as does my snipping of corrupted flesh.

"Wanderer."

It's my turn to smile.

"Names are a dangerous thing, I suppose," he says, peering down at the shears with contempt while I remove the final piece.

"Ain't that the truth?"

"I wonder if perhaps I already know your name, Purveyor."

Biting the silver, I look up and match his piercing glare. His head twists, as though looking beyond my weathered, leathery skin. When you get to my age, the ravages of time hide a man more effectively than shadow, but regardless, I can smell the intrigue burning within him. The hunt for memories lost. Of a forgotten nemesis, or the familiar scent of enemies past. Do I know him? Surely not. But as with any great mountain, it's so easy to forget the stones that built and made it so. How many corpses have built mine? How many unseen toes have I stepped on in my years of killing? Might as well count the bloody stars for all the time it would take you.

Razor claws drum the surface of the table beside my face.

My fingers burn for the silver at my back.

"You are no ordinary human, Purveyor. To kneel before me so, to hold your heartbeat steady." His black tongue dances dangerously around a fang. "Yes... You are someone, or perhaps you were in another life. Someone fearsome." His eyes burn with ancient power, dimming even the candlelight glowing about the room. "Yes..."

"I'm nobody," I respond flatly, folding over an off-white rag of clean cloth. "Just a merchant trying to make ends meet."

"Oh? And what would a nobody be doing with this amongst his wares?" He holds up a golden clasp shaped like the head of a bat, a snarl of fangs set beneath a pair of blood red rubies for eyes.

My throat tightens, but I don't let it show. "Just something I picked up along the way." A blatant lie, but he doesn't know that.

The vampire barks a laugh. "Nobody simply 'picks up' a crest of the Vandervel's, my dear man. They are elder blood, one and all. A bloodline whose fangs harrowed the furthest reaches of the continent once upon a time. No. You are something more than you make out to be. A Blade of Ruin, perhaps, long in the tooth and weary to the bone?"

"You looking to find out, friend?"

Silence returns, a battle waged unblinking between us. By any measure, he should have me dead to rights, but there is an unknown that would make any smart man think twice. I could be a useless old bastard, or I could be holding an ace between my butt cheeks. Question is, will he pay to find out? I know he's feeling me out, but if he wants to grab my arse, he'd better be ready to kiss his hand goodbye.

The corners of his lips tug to reveal those bony fangs, but the malevolent glow of his gaze subsides. He turns away.

"No," he says, dropping the crest onto the table with a thud. "Now is not the time. But I can feel it, you know?"

"Hm?"

"That disc of silver hidden beneath your clothes. The mark of your kind."

The base of my stomach crumbles, an abyss yawning wide beneath. My patient gives me a sidelong stare.

"You would do well to remove it if you wish to cater to those you have destroyed, lest you invite our wrath into your home."

I say nothing. I've never heard of such a sense. Not among the lesser bloods. Perhaps this one is older than I gave him credit for. Were he not weak from his injury, he would surely turn me into a snack.

The Wanderer lifts his hand in an airy wave, like he'd commented on no more than the weather.

"Just food for thought, my friend."

I don't answer, instead opting to change the subject. Picking up the bandage, I try to think of something a merchant would say.

"How did you come by this place?" I ask, grasping at straws.

"The blood on the sign," he replies, wincing as I dig back in to my work. "I could—Ah."

"Sorry."

"I could smell it on the wind when I made my way down from the mountain pass. I must say, it was a nice touch."

"From that far? Even with the wind, I didn't expect it to carry to the mountain."

"Indeed. Though I must admit, my senses have been particularly keen tonight. I am correct in thinking it is the same for your kind, no? When one is hungry, a drop of blood might as well be a pitcher."

"Hmph. Makes sense, I suppose." The things you learn. Such information would've been useful all those years ago. None of my teachings or findings revealed such a thing, yet it makes sense for any species that must feed. In the recesses of my mind, I quietly wonder what else I don't know about my lifelong enemies.

Danger subsiding, I pop the cork stopper on the vial, soaking the off-white rag until it is stained brackish black and foul-smelling. The poison of the Dread Mother tingles on my skin, but my tolerance is far greater than that of the average human.

"Water of the Mother," the vampire says, still watching from the corner of his eye. "Interesting."

The hairs stand up on the nape of my neck. So much for secrets. Now there's nothing to keep him from attacking me, and he already has plenty of reason to do so. I wash over the wound hastily, making him wince, then fold the rag into a neat square and tell him to hold it against his wound. He does so, and I wrap the bandage around his waist, quickly tying it off beneath his jerkin so I can stand the hell up.

"You should be fine in a few days," I say, trying to cover my alarm.

"Thank you. Your services are most welcome, if a little unexpected. Now, I recall there being a mention of blood earlier?"

"There was."

He spreads his pale palms wide. "Only, I fear I have run out of coin."

I sigh. Guess this is also going to be on the house. I could refuse, but is that wise?

"I can offer you something better than gold." The Wanderer smirks.

"Such as?"

"A promise."

"My favourite form of guarantee. Someone's word."

"It is not someone's word you shall have," the Wanderer

snaps. "It is *my* word. And that is worth more than you know."

"I'm listening. What do you propose?"

"My protection. When I deem you need it most. You seem capable enough, but should the need and opportunity arise, I shall act in your interest."

"Sounds hit or miss. What if I end up dead when I need you most?"

"Then I promise to bring you back to life instead. Better than new, I might add."

That sends a shiver down my spine. "Do me one better?"

"Go on."

"If I die, promise not to bring me back, okay?"

The Wanderer offers a conscientious nod. "Agreed."

Honestly isn't half bad. Reckon if I'm ever getting fucked, there's maybe a one-in-four chance he'll get me unfucked. Maybe. Could be worse. He could be getting me fucked right this very minute. And not in the way I like it, either. Not wanting to give sod's law a chance, I make my move. "If you're just bear with me, I'll prepare some fresh blood for you."

A warm comfort glazes over his features, like a ravenous traveller promised a meal of cheese and bread. Anything will do when you are hungry.

"Excellent."

"Can I trust you to behave while I pour it for you?"

"Certainly." He waves his hand nonchalantly, the aristocratic tone returning post-haste. "One of my standing does not simply discard proper etiquette."

The response comes easily, but I don't like the cut of his smile. Jagged like a rusty blade's edge. He appears relaxed in the chair, but something about him is poised. Like a cat, relaxing in close proximity to a mouse, ready to pounce.

I move across the room to the cupboard and withdraw a small copper goblet. "I'll just go fetch your drink."

"I will be waiting."

Hopefully, that's all you'll be doing. Moving into the hallway, I step back onto the empty shop floor and place the goblet on the counter, then stare at my knife. A cut to my arm would be less annoying to deal with in the coming days. It would also take forever to bleed without going deeper than I'm willing to go. The palm of the hand just bleeds a damn sight faster, and I'm in no desperate need to make this take any longer than necessary.

"Sod it." I growl, gripping the blade in my hand and pulling. It slices open the flesh of my palm, burning it cold, then hot, the air stinging deep. My skin tingles. Hot blood flows freely. I clench my fist over the goblet and squeeze, the crimson running fast. It shouldn't take more than a minute or two.

Laboured breaths catch my ear, raking a finger of ice down my spine. I crane my neck around. See the elder blood standing in the doorway gripping the frame, his chest heaving like he'd been running for a week. His blood-red eyes flash to my hand, fangs baring in a ferocious snarl.

"I cannot wait any longer." He snarls, his voice edged with the demonic. I try to turn around, but he flies at me with inhuman speed. We crash to the floor in a scattering of twisted limbs, his razor-bladed fangs gnashing at my throat.

I wrap my bloody hand around his neck, trying to hold him back, but the smell of blood sends him into a frenzy. He snaps and thrashes, buckling my arm. I draw the knife up and slash him across the cheek, his skin hissing like pork crackling as it carves across the bone. He yelps, writhing away, my slick grip lost on his throat. He looks at his own bloody palm, then back to me with feral hunger. Lunging, his claws are raised high and wide. I draw my feet between us as he falls upon me, and I kick him against the wall with everything I have. My hip screams a wail of pain that drowns out all else. The adrenaline pumping through my veins helps me move faster than I have in years. Spurring me to my feet, I charge into him, my knife tip spearing for his heart.

His eyes widen, and so does mine. I thrust my hand down, stabbing him in the wound I'd just bloody dressed. Skin crackles and pops at the touch of the silver blade, making him cry out in agony. He pulls away, a plume of smoke escaping the wound when my knife drags free, the blade coated in dark, coagulated blood.

We both drop to the floor on our knees, aching to the bone.

"Sorry," I say quickly, wiping blood from my lip, though I don't remember him hitting me. Must've happened in the fall. Now whose chest is heaving.

"I hope this doesn't... affect future business... between us," I manage between ragged gasps. "I don't have many customers right now."

The Wanderer shoots me a baffled look, then checks his side, buckling.

"No. No, I forget myself. Forgive me."

"Forgiven." I wave it off, painfully hauling myself to my feet. Did throwing down like this always hurt so damn much? I knew I was old, but Night Mother be damned. I brush myself off and straighten myself up, pleased with the lack of dust on the floor. "If you'll behave for a minute longer, your drink will soon be ready."

The Wanderer heaves himself up to sitting, resting lethargically against the back wall. He dabs at his scorched cheek with his wrist and checks it, then lets his head fall back onto the wooden boards. "That would be most welcome."

Back on my feet, I hobble towards the counter. The goblet sits where I left it, almost a quarter full. Guess that's something. I gaze at my hand, now smeared with red, and clench it into a fist over the goblet, working the flow back into a steady drip. All around us, blood coats the floor, the walls, and the counter. Anyone would think it was a damn blood bath in here.

To my side, my guest is busy running a finger through a handprint of blood, then sticks it in his mouth and sucks. His lids close heavily, a sense of relief washing over his face. He must be weak from his run-in with the Blade that caught up to him, else he would've killed me with little difficulty back there. It's a sobering thought, but not as poignant as the unexpected guilt creeping into my chest. What would my brothers say if they knew I was helping the enemy? Most would probably shrug in silence. We all understand the way of the world, eventually. Some sooner than others, but in the end, you either figure it out or die trying. Nothing really changes. Good, evil? Just a crock of shit. Survival is really all there is.

"How is that drink coming?"

I break from my pathetic justifications for my betrayal and look down into the goblet. It's filled two-thirds of the way. Maybe I cut a little too deep after all.

"Ready." I grab a clean cloth from under the counter partition and wrap it around my hand to staunch the flow. I'll dump some yarrow on it later. Dress it properly. For now, I've a customer to attend.

Taking the goblet in my bad hand, I hobble over, leading with my good leg, and hold out my other hand to help him up.

He regards me warily, almost confused. Can't say I blame him, but this is my job now. He doesn't take it, instead climbing to his feet with all the dignity a tired sucker can muster and then takes the proffered goblet.

"Thank you," he whispers, staring at the crimson liquid with ravenous lust. He slurps it down greedily, his spine stiffening while he drinks, until not a drop is left. Only the drips running down the sides of his mouth remain. Two ruby red fangs.

"Ahh... Heaven, Devil forgive me." He wipes his mouth with the side of his hand and licks that up, too. "Thank you, Purveyor."

"Any time. I suppose I'll have to patch those holes back up." I gesture, drawing his attention to his wound.

"Oh, that." He drums his fingers on the goblet, pondering. "Will it fester again?"

"Shouldn't do. Silver wasn't in there long enough this time."

"Indeed. Do not concern yourself, Purveyor. I shall be fine."

"Very well. I'll give you some spare bandages in case you change your mind."

"No, no. Save them for next time."

"If you're sure." I shrug, feeling a little cheap. "Will you be needing anything else tonight?"

The vampire glances around the room, a hairless brow raising. "No. No, I believe I have everything I need. I appreciate your help. This has been... interesting, to say the least."

"To say the least. Forgive me for asking but, you wouldn't happen to be chasing someone, would you?"

He scrutinises my face, searching my expression. "Someone?"

"Someone..." I gesture with a roll of the hand. "A skittish man with a mane of brown hair and old clothes."

"Oh. Certainly not one of mine, but you have been good to me. If I come across him, do you want me to bleed him dry?"

"No," I say quickly, shaking my head. "Nothing like that. He was jumping at shadows, and when I asked who was chasing him, he insisted that to utter the name would bring his assailant barrelling through the void upon us. With the way you arrived, I thought maybe it was you."

"What name must not be uttered?"

"Was hoping you could tell me. He called it the Dark One."

The vampire shrugs as if to say it is all the same to him, then freezes, his expression twisting in thought.

"Dark One? Was this skittish man alive?"

"Flesh and blood, same as me. Even mentioned the fact, as it happens."

My customer nods slowly, looking me up and down like he'd only just met me. "Yes... Yes, I see now. How did I not see it sooner?"

"See what?"

Gingerly, he glances around the room, lingering upon the shadows. "I would prefer not to say, only... do you have more candles?"

A lump of concern festers deep in my gut. What on Earth would have an elder blood twitching at the window curtain so?

"Well, I had best be off. Who knows when that pesky sun will rise? It seems to come earlier every night."

"Ain't that the truth?"

"Yes," he says, studying me for a moment. "I can show myself out."

He hastily adjusts his cloak on his shoulders before taking another long survey of the room, then turns back to me. "Maybe I'll visit the sights in that village down the hill. Maybe..."

I don't reply to that. It's none of my business. Not anymore. Although... "The family living in the water mill chop my wood," I hasten to add.

"Is that so? Well, I never did much like water. Too thin for my tastes." The vampire strides to the door, apparently not used to such an exit. He looks back, perhaps checking for a crossbow aimed at his back, and then pulls the door from its frame, eliciting a splintery wail as a gusty wind bellows through the crack.

"Farewell, Purveyor."

"Until next time," I call. "Oh!"

"Yes?" the Wanderer asks, turning around sharply. He really is on edge, but is it me he's worried about, or what I told him? Either way...

"Won't you take a flyer? Share it with your friends, perhaps?"

He glances down at the iron table by the door, the red candles glowing beside the stack.

"C—Certainly," he says, peeling one from the top with a dainty pinch and giving it the once over. He nods to himself, then folds it and tucks it beneath his cloak. And with that he makes his exit, the front door creaking closed behind him, the little brass bell singing mournfully above.

The wisps of wind are starved, and the shop falls silent. Tiredness sweeps over me, the adrenaline of our encounter ebbing away. I scoop the coins from my pocket and count them. Four copper bits. Not bad, I suppose, for a cut hand and a little Water of the Mother. Hardly worth entering in the damn book at all. I grab a tablecloth and spit on the coins. No need to leave them bloody. It isn't my business, that. Not anymore. At least I keep telling myself. So why do I feel otherwise? Old habits die hard, I guess.

It's my turn to take a long, hard look around the shop floor. Pockets of shadow still cluster in the small spaces, just beyond light's reach. Outside, the wind moans again like a banshee mourning its lost lover. I Can't help grumbling under my breath. I really need to have a little sit-down chat with my assistant and his somewhat understandable habits. But first...

"I'm gonna need some more sodding candles."

CHAPTER NINE

FLAMING SPLINT IN HAND, the final candle atop my bloodworm counter takes flame, completing my grand design of replicating the sun right here on my own shop floor. Take the walls off this place, and it would shine from here to the Dragon Spires and beyond, a blistering beacon in the choked darkness; and a burning vista no creature of the night would ever dare set foot upon. Bad for business, that. Fortunately, the howling storm would snuff out every candle in an instant. Not that the walls are going to disappear anytime soon.

I don't know why I'm even blabbering on about this. Call it delirium, having been denied my medicine for so many long hours into the night. It makes me wonder how I ever survived long hunts out in the field, cut off from my one true love in life. Oh, who am I kidding? Those hip flasks were so filled to the brim they damn near dragged me to a watery grave on three separate occasions. Still, I would've succumbed much sooner without their fiery touch to warm my bones.

I blow the flame from the splint's end, leaving a cool

ember and a thin trail of smoke to disperse lazily into the air. It took a lot of careful positioning, but my entire emporium is lit up like a sodding pyre. It's honestly a little too bright, and by that, I mean I'm on the verge of having my retinas seared clean off. Though it wouldn't be the worst thing that's ever happened to me. I once had a dream the wife cut my nuts off with cheese wire. It had me flinching at shadows for a month. She would do it, too. She once caught me cheating on her with the washerwoman who, incidentally, didn't wash. The fact that it was just another of her insecure dreams didn't seem to matter much. I spent damn-near two weeks walking around with one hand guarding the family line. Or the possibility of one at any rate. Still... They were good times.

I wipe my eyes before they can tear up, growling a curse at my stock supply. It must be the garlic wafting something fierce in the far corner of the room, stinging my eyes. Idiots love that shit for warding off vampires. I once saw a guy wrapping a wreath of the stuff around his sack before taking a bath in a puddle. He had his priorities right, that one. Not that garlic does sod all. Just don't tell the punters that or it would cause bloody bedlam.

Turning towards the hall, I head for my bedchamber door, for it to dawn on me that the precarious state of the world is somewhat laughable. Peasants buy garlic to ward off vampires, while vampire hunters tell them to do the very same, selling the stuff in droves. Then on the flip side, you've got half the vampire caste acting like it actually works, just so the peasants don't come up with something more effective. Laughable... more like disgusting.

In all my years of hunting, I never once span that yarn to anyone. But now I'm a business owner, and it's my duty to stock what the customers want, whether they need it or not.

It isn't any of my business what they spend their ill-begotten coin on. Shit; if I didn't sell it, they would call me the idiot.

Having lit every corner of my entire home, I once again find myself wondering where my moonlighting assistant has wandered off to. In fairness, he's done a fair bit of work, and brought in a fair bit of coin, too. I can't blame him for that, but that sure as shit doesn't excuse him from raiding my precious booze supply. It's about damn time we took a seat and had a talk. Man to man.

Bolstered by my pep talk, I begin the arduous task of tracking the devil down. He's done well to evade me so far, but no longer. It's time to lay down the law. Show him who the boss around here really is.

I start by checking each room, expecting to find him lurking in a brightly lit corner with a drunken smile on his lips. Just the thought of it really puts my back up, and I pick up the pace. He's not in the bedchamber. Peeking into the stockroom, he isn't there either. He wasn't on the shop floor last I looked, so that means... I turn to the nearby window in the hall and peer out into the lashing rain. I don't much feel like going out in the shit, but sometimes a man has got to act. Lead from the front. Forward thinking and all the crap. And speaking of forward thinking, an idea strikes me. The mirror. I return to the bedchamber, sweeping over the furs on the bed for where I cast it aside. Gone.

"The fuck?"

It's not on the floor, nor under the bed, either. Did he take it? Maybe he wants to keep me from checking up on him. Crafty old bastard. Well, if he thinks that will deter me, he doesn't know me very well... which seems rather unlikely, given the circumstances. I guess I'll just have to find him without it. That's what it means to be a boss, after all. Problem solving on the fly.

Mustering up enough boss-man courage to face the lashing rain, I return to the shop floor and pull the front door open, staring beyond my porch into the heart of the storm. Why the hell anyone would want to be out in this is beyond me.

Out on the slick grass, the priest's body wagon sits lonely in the cold, though it's not where I left it. Strange. Did my assistant turn it around? I can't imagine why he would, but then, I've been known to do some stupid things in my time, even by my standards. Perhaps he's gone out back again, pissing into the abyss, or doing who knows what else.

Not wanting to brace the biting rain, I close the door and walk to my bedchamber, unbolt the back door and disarm the thunder scrolls, lest I clap my own arse by mistake. The door creaks open with an unruly moan, unleashing the storm upon my home and peppering my face with shards of icy rain. I bundle my arms against the cold and push out into the night, looking towards the outhouse and the well. Nothing.

A slam behind me damn near makes me leap from my skin. Turning around, I can see the back door has closed. This bastarding wind has me jumping at ghosts. I'm about ready to call it quits when I notice the stable door slightly ajar. It's not where I left it, but again, it could just be the wind. I suppose I'll never know unless I check. Maybe he's disposing of the body for me. Now that would be the bloody day.

Fighting through the howling storm, tongues of long grass lap at my ankles and darken the brown of my boots to dusky night. I remind myself, I've suffered worse in my time, though in the moment it rarely feels like it. A few more bitter paces, and I'm at the broken door, pulling it wide to peer inside the inky darkness.

"You in here?" I call out, craning my head around the door to peer at the dead body I stashed out of sight earlier in the night. Either the dead bastard has bloated to five times his size, or I'm staring at a pile of dead people. I blink away the dark and edge in deeper, leaving the rain behind. My mind does backflips, trying to discern the large silhouetted mound before me. It *is* a pile of bodies. But who—

I grab the shoulder of one, rolling over a slim frame. The hard-eyed girl, and my assistant's first customer, stares lifelessly, her features frozen in shock. My eyes adjust to the low light, and I can make out the bloody trail carved across her neck, and the dark stain running down her chest. The cogs in my mind turn, and suddenly it all makes sense.

"Oh, shit."

What have I done? I've unleashed a bloody monster. I swallow hard; the hairs raising on the back of my neck, my voice barely a croaked whisper. "I've unleashed me."

I turn and dash from the stable, running around the side of my emporium to the front as fast as my legs will carry me. I've got to stop him before he kills the wrong person. Bodies leave questions, and the only people that answer them are at the sharp end of the law. Leaping onto my porch, I clamber for the door handle with both hands, when my own voice spills from the darkness at my side.

"Looking for something?" my assistant asks from beyond my sight. Claws of icy warning rake down my back. I whip around to see him lounging in my rocking chair in the shadows of my porch, his mirror resting in his hand. So that's where it went. "I've been doing some looking myself, and I've discovered something."

"Oh, yeah?" I fold my arms, bracing off the gathering chill, completely out of position and on the back foot. "What's that, then?"

"That we need to talk." He gestures to the stool that wasn't there before, and for reasons unknown, I obey.

"Okay?" I mutter, sliding uncomfortably into the seat. It's too low, and my knees point up awkwardly, making me feel like a schoolboy before the headmaster. Pretty sure he found it in the damn stable. It's probably used for milking cows or torturing people by making them sit on the bloody thing. "So, what's the problem?"

My assistant's mouth pinches around my pipe, making the corner of my eye twitch. He exhales slowly; the smoke billowing from his nostrils to taint the air. It smells like autumn leaves. I've been looking for that fucking thing all night long. I realise he's nursing a bottle of amber liquor, too. The good stuff, as it happens. *My* good stuff. The dark glass, almost unseen in the shroud of night, reflects the pipe's sombre glow from its perch upon the side table. On his lap rests the store ledger, open to the first page.

"What's this all about?" I ask, feeling hot under the collar. Which, quite frankly, is fucking ludicrous.

"I've been reviewing the sales," my assistant says with another sweeping gesture over the darkened pages. "Doing some... accounting."

"Oh? And what of it?"

He takes another drag, the bowl-fire illuminating his unwavering eyes in the darkness. The oppressive gaze of a hard man used to doing hard things. Peculiarly, it sends a coil of tension down my spine, and I don't quite know where to look. Is this what it's like for others that deal with me? I've never been on this side of the interrogation before.

He pulls the pipe from his lips and sighs a dusky cloud, tapping his finger on the side of the bowl. "Someone's been dipping into the strongbox."

"What?"

"Skimming off the top," he continues, pausing for emphasis. "What do you make of that?"

It's my turn to drum fingers. The headmaster vanishes before my eyes, now more akin to an inquisitor of the Chain, asking questions with my nuts in a vice, and he's just begging for a reason to squeeze.

"Not sure what to make of it," I say truthfully, thinking back over the night. "You sure you counted right?"

"Positive."

A flash of irritation burns hot behind my cheeks. First, he smokes my stash, then he drinks the good stuff. Now he's accusing me of stealing from myself.

"You got something to say, just say it." I growl, feeling the fire growing inside. "Don't jerk my chain, boy."

"Fine. I'll say it." He slams the ledger closed. "You're robbing this business blind, old man. Killing customers before they've bought a damn thing, while letting others go scot-free."

I open my mouth to retort, but he beats me to it.

"Throwing precious wood on the fire like summer never ends, sleeping on the job, selling valuable maps to some wanker paying in hopes and dreams. You're a liability, and if I keep letting you get away with it, not only will this store not make it off the ground, but we ain't gonna make it through winter."

"That right."

"It is."

"You got proof, boy?"

My assistant throws something at me, and my instincts pluck it from the air before I can register what's coming my way. I turn my hand and stare at the small purse I pulled off the priest at the start of the night.

"What the—"

"Open it."

I frown at that, pulling the drawstring loose and dumping out the contents. A single gold coin falls into the palm of my hand, precious metal cool to the touch.

He gives me a cold stare. "How much you got there?"

"One gold piece," I shoot back, concern welling within me. How does he know about this? It wasn't even written down in the damn book.

"One. Gold. Piece." My assistant shakes his head slowly. "Far cry from five, wouldn't you say?"

"Wha—" That stops me in my tracks. How the hell does he know? I made this transaction before he even arrived, goddamnit. But then it hits me, and I have to refrain from slapping myself on the sodding forehead.

"Did you forget?" he asks, tapping the pipe on the heel of his boot before stowing it in his pocket. He places the book down on the side table beside the bottle, then climbs to stand over me, fingers rising to tap his temple. "I know everything."

Anger gorges in my throat, but before I can unleash a vicious rebuke, my imposter throws the empty bottle at me. He snatches something from his back, lunging at me with murder in his eyes.

I try to rise. On instinct, I deflect the bottle. Instead, I catch his wrist, the sting of traitorous silver poised to bury beneath my eye. Without thinking, I unleash its twin, stabbing mercilessly at the man who would become me.

He, too, catches my wrist with practiced ease. We tumble to the hard porch floor and spill over the edge into the wet grass, their cold tongues lashing at my neck and arms. We roll, and suddenly I'm on top of him. I lean down with everything I have in a desperate bid to kill myself. To say such an intent is unsettling would be a gross understatement, but I have no other choice.

"You never wanted to succeed." My double hisses through clenched teeth. His elbow is stuck hard against the floor to keep my blade from sinking any closer to his heart.

"I *can* do this," I bark back, more at myself than anyone else. Quite literally.

His grimace twists into a malicious snarl, his eyes bulging with defiance. "You don't have the guts, old man."

Before I can prove him wrong, he throws us sideways, rolling and swiping in a tangle of limbs. Trails of fire tear along my side in the battle for purchase, warmth spilling through my clothes and running to my hip. Flesh wound. Ignore it. It's the ones you can't feel you need to worry about.

We land in reversed roles. But before he can take another stab, I punch him square in the face with everything I have. His skin unnaturally ripples like a stone cast into an otherworldly lake. I might not be the supplest old man around, but that isn't normal even for me.

"I don't think so." He grins from behind my fist, unfazed, his blade rising. I drag my knee up between us and lever my foe over my head, sending him tumbling over the grass with concerning grace. He's no joke. He really is me. I can't risk fighting this arsehole straight up. I need an advantage.

In a flash, my would-be murderer rolls to his feet, spinning to receive me. Only I'm not there. Instead, I'm legging it through a wash of burning agony in my mad dash for the front door. I wrench the handle and throw myself inside. Venomous footfalls are close at my back, the blinding light within scorching my vision with blistering yellow light.

Squinting against shadow's bane, I scan the shop floor in a bid for anything that might aid me. Something to give me that edge. The wall of weapons is useless to me. Heavy iron and old steel, none of which can hold a candle to a deft hand wielding silver alloy. I dash down the opposite side of the room, eying the various potions when the creak of a crossbow string catches my ear, sending my stomach into free-fall so bad, I might have just shit myself.

Desperate, I grab a round vial of festered swamp bile. It's a hideous concoction that can expand many times its volume when agitated and makes a ten-day sweaty arse crack smell like roses by comparison. Twisting around, I hold the vial brew up high, spotting my double with a bolt of iron levelled at my chest. Why in the hell didn't I think of that?

My would-be murderer's eyes widen at the sight, his steel resolve reduced to brittle slag.

"Hold it!" He lowers the crossbow and reaches out a pleading hand. "You pop that thing in here and cleaning the mess will be worse than death."

"Yeah?" I cradle the vial precariously between my thumb and forefinger. It's poised to smash into a thousand pieces of fuck you all over my nice hardwood floor. "Well, you'd better think twice about pulling that trigger then, hadn't you? Tosser."

"You're bluffing," my double says, licking his lips dangerously, the metal in his voice returning. "You haven't cleaned a goddamn thing since I got here. You ain't gonna make that kind of mess."

"Then why haven't you pulled the trigger, arsehole? Do it." Now I really am bluffing, but this is me we're dealing with here. Neither of us is going to back down without a fight.

He clenches his jaw, his options running through his mind. He knows I'm petty enough to die just to spite him, and there's no way on God's green earth I'm going clean this shit up if it blows; therefore, I can only assume that neither will he. I've got all my eggs in one basket, but he's got me by the short and curlies. What else can I do?

"Okay, listen," he says finally, the deadly bolt lowering once more. "There are cleaner ways to do this. I spent hours organising that fucking table you're about to shit all over, so how about a mutual reset?"

I cock an eyebrow at that. All things considered, it isn't a bad deal. "Fine. Lose the crossbow, and I'll put the vial back."

A scowl corrupts my double's face, but he reluctantly agrees. "Fine."

He makes to chuck the crossbow, when I halt him in his tracks.

"Hold it. Bolt one way. Crossbow the other."

He smiles at that. "Thought you were gonna let that one slip for a second there."

"Not on your grave, old man."

"Uh, huh? We'll see about that." He dislodges the bolt and chucks it towards the weapon studded wall, before sliding the crossbow towards the potions. "Happy?"

"Not exactly the first word that springs to mind, but it's a start."

Careful not to lose sight of my dubious foe, I reluctantly replace the blasphemous potion back on the shelf with its multi-coloured array of brothers and sisters, when I spot something that simply cannot be.

"Hang on," I say, fishing another vial from the shelf and holding it out for him to see. "This is whisperfang anti-venom."

My double folds his arms, shifting on the spot. "So?"

"So, you sold the last vial."

"Yeah, well, it's not like he's gonna need it now, is it?"

I slap my forehead in disbelief. This bastard's been killing the clientele and putting their paid goods back up for sale this whole time! It's brilliant, and clearly a trait he got from me. I replace the vial, an audible sigh expelling from my ex-assistant.

"Ready?" he asks, shrugging awkwardly.

I glance around, shifting towards the pile of dried garlic cloves and taking a fistful. "Ready."

Garlic flies from my fingers, peppering the bastard in relentless handfuls of ineffective destruction.

"Oh, you—Ow. Stop!"

But my hands keep on pumping, unleashing every vampire killer's worst nightmare upon the freshly swept shop floor; more garlic than you can shake your bloody stake at. A clove nails him on the dome, bouncing helplessly out of sight.

"Son of a bitch!" My imposter snatches up a halberd that growls a merciless ring, the vicious length of iron levelled and ready to skewer me and my army of cloves.

"Shit." Why didn't I grab one of those?

He charges down the central aisle, lighting a fire under my arse. I restock with another fistful of cloves and dive at the nearby table, circling it to keep the bastard out of striking range.

"Come here!"

"Like fuck."

I throw another clove, my confidence levels peeling worse than the bloody garlic. This really stinks. I dash left as he tries to head me off, then I switch back again. My eyes searching. Left wanting. He sweeps the blade over the table, but I pull back. Ducking beneath the table, he rakes the blade at my ankles. I barely manage to jump in time. Surprised I even did it at all. Not bad for an old man.

He pops back up, a foul grimace on his face from across the assorted sea of knock-off wares, when something catches my eye. Something I hadn't noticed until now, but it had been driving me nuts all the same.

"Hang on," I snap, holding up the last of my deadly payload. "You stacked the polearms all wrong on the rack."

"Wha—No I never." He switches right, glowering at the racks of weapons closest to the door. "Ah—"

"Ah is right." I tut. "It's been driving me bloody mental trying to figure out what you did wrong."

"*I* did wrong?" he spits back at me, his shoulders bunching. "What have *you* done?"

I lift my arms up, looking around at everything before us. "Take your pick. Now, are you going to sort that rack, or do I have to do it when you're dead?"

"Oh, bollocks it all." My double snarls, leaning his halberd against the table and pulling out his—my—pipe. "You're not going to do it even if you do win, and knowing that will keep me up in the next life, knowing my sodding luck."

"What luck," I start, offended.

"Exactly! Just let me have a tug on this while I do it."

"Oi." I scratch my arm, feeling an intense need. "Fine, you've convinced me. I'll help, but you're sharing that damn bowl."

He looks at me like I've accosted his good person, which is pretty bloody rich.

"You're lucky I'm sharing with you at all," I remind him.

"Such luck." My double flippantly waves his hand, puffing the bowl alight and moves towards the rack.

I drop my cloves on the table and join him, rattling the

spears and glaives from their nooks and rearranging them into their proper order.

"Here." He hands me the pipe.

"Thanks." I accept, biting down on the bit while I work a stubborn pole into an overly tight hole. He didn't even have them arranged by height. Honestly, you just can't get the help these days.

"Quit your bitching, old man."

The glaive slots in and I take the pipe from my lips, a dense cloud of satisfaction swirling in my lungs and rejuvenating my senses.

"What?" I ask, releasing sweet relief into the air as he snatches the pipe from my clutches. "I didn't say anything."

"Didn't have to," he shoots back, shuffling like it's his last.

"Fair."

He kicks the bowl out on his heel and replaces it in his pocket, still gripping the last spear. "All done," he says, exhaling a breath.

"Not exactly," I point out, eying the spear.

"Oh, this?" He levels the head at me, releasing a cold drip of sweat down my temple. "This one's for me."

"Shit."

I turn on my heels, racing across the store and flying through the counter partition, falling below the old wood as the spear stabs over the top. My knees burn from the impact, but I keep crawling for the hallway door, the looming shadow blotting out the floor from above. I twist around. See the angel of death hovering overhead, his spear ready to plunge. It's a peculiar sight.

"Say goodnight, old man." He stabs a lethal blow, but I throw myself sideways, punching my back against the wall and hurting my ribs. Fuck it. I squish myself low to dodge another swipe. Heat drags across the back of my calf. I'll take it.

"Come back here," echoes fierce words. I scarper into the hallway, scrambling onto my feet and dashing for the stockroom door. "You can't escape yourself!"

Wise words, but like hell, I'm going to listen. And speaking of hell, why I would want to go into that particular hole evades me even now. Truthfully, it's my only hope. I need that edge.

Gripping the door handle, I stare back down the candlelit hallway in the hopes of a miracle.

The shadow of death appears on the wall, followed by the worst assistant I've ever had. Fuck it. It's now or never. I swallow hard and push the stockroom door open, ducking back inside to the Devil's playroom. God help me…

I know she won't.

CHAPTER TEN

I KICK the stockroom door open and dash inside, then grab the first thing I see to protect myself from the thunderous footfalls of the imposter assassin hounding my back. A self-lighting candle that refuses to be held the right way up. Fucking typical! The light in here is weak, despite the candle's ember-cracked hearth and the guttered candles lining the walls. Desperate, I search for anything better suited to my survival than a temperamental stick with a bad attitude. Scanning the piles of freshly organised trinkets and scrolls, I realise I have no more idea now about what is placed where, than when it was one great collective shit heap.

"There you are, you bastard."

I whip around, staring at the ominous silhouette standing in the doorway, the stupid upside-down candle scuffing my vision in the low light.

"Thought you could get away, did you?" he said. "You and I both know there's no salvation in here."

I glance at the chained vase on the mantelpiece, knowing exactly what that smart-arse is getting at.

"No better for me than it is for you," I counter, throwing the candle at him and edging back deeper into the room, the defiant candle bouncing off the floor and levitating in mid-air between us, as though possessed by some overly obnoxious spirit.

My murderous clone breaches the doorway, his dark eyes leaden with that killer's stare. I grope for anything that might aid me in my plight. A sudden and somewhat misplaced wave of sympathy washes over me for all those I have hunted over the long years. I'm still at least half the man I once was, but despite that, I find my nuts crawling up inside my stomach while staring down this devil in the dark. I'm every bit the killer he is, yet I can't help but feel like the sheep before the wolf. That the only thing in this hellish life able to kill me is myself, fills me with an odd sense of pride.

"I know what you're thinking," growls the voice that is not my own. "Know what you're doing."

I slide behind the round table, creating another barrier between us.

"You want an advantage," he says, simmering and edging closer to the table. "Anything but to suffer a fair fight. It's how you've survived all these long years. Lurking in uncertainty. Killing from the cover of darkness."

"Goddamn right. And I would do it again."

"You're not a man. You're a coward. Nothing but a cutthroat in the night, not worth the scum beneath my boots."

"Like you would do it different?" I shoot back, my irritation flaring.

"Damn right I wouldn't. I'm you, after all. A pathetic wimp in the night."

Rather than bite his head off, I decide to blow it off instead. I grab one of the deadly breaker scrolls from my table, unleashing unknown power into my home without a care for the otherworldly destruction it may wrought.

"Shut up and die, you pipe pilfering shit rag!"

A flurry of feathers burst from the page as chickens erupt from the scroll, flapping wings and clucking chaos around the tiny room. I grit my teeth in terror, snapping my gaze to the stone vase in which ultimate evil sleeps; petrified that such a racket will stir the depths of destruction into an uncontainable fury.

"How *dare* you!" my double bellows from across the table. His fit of outrage whips me back to see his knock-off, tunic-wearing arse covered in a sizzling splat of fried egg. The yoke, a perfect sun of tasty orange, makes my stomach rumble something fierce. My double lunges over the table and grabs another of the breaker scrolls. He unfurls the parchment with not a care about the disastrous consequences that might be contained within.

My butthole puckers. The enigmatic scrawl of red ink coating the old parchment ignites like burning coals. Its surface ripples like water. Something peers from beneath the warping surface. My heart begins to thunder before the pink and fleshy monstrosity emerges from realms unseen.

In a burst of speed, the creature soars from the parchment with a deafening squeal. Its ears flop in the air, and its sunken eyes are afeared behind a bulbous protruding snout. It hits the table with a wood-splintering thud, scrambling cleft hooves—nay—trotters, through the ocean of unidentified relics littering the table in a bid to escape, its meaty visage riddled with rasher-shaped cuts and missing sections of rib. With a mighty oink, the foul creature hefts its sizeable bulk onto its skinny legs, scarpering from the tabletop with an ear-splitting squeal. A trail of sausage links firing from its arse with such voracity, it stun-locks the both of us into a triple-take.

"What in the world?" we both mumble, utterly bewildered. I've seen some things, but *this* is something beyond even my jaded expectations. Fortunately, my would-be assassin appears more confounded than I, for my hand reaches another nearby scroll before he can do the same, and in my bid for victory, I unleash its power without a second thought.

Spotting my gambit, my double shrinks away. His eyes widen with fear when something oddly potato shaped fires across the room and punches him in the gut. It explodes in a cluster of baton-shaped yellow sticks that cascade through the air in a fizzle of golden brown.

"Ouch, that—"

But his cry is lost in the carb-infested hailstorm of exploding potatoes pinging mercilessly across the tabletop battlefield. Deep piggy grunts cut through the clamour as the startled beast runs laps around the room, entangling us in more sausage-links than an understaffed pig farmer on market day.

Arcing the parchment toward my double as he throws himself through the air in a bid to escape the starchy onslaught, my gaze settles on the remaining scrolls lying before me, and the worn ribbon that binds them. Suddenly, it dawns on me. These are not breaker scrolls at all. They're breakfast scrolls!

An affronted cluck cries out. My attention is snapped to the scene of something falling from up above in another puff of feathers. A stunned chicken, free-falling behind the table, with a potato wedged to its beak.

"Oops." I redirect the fire, pinging spuds off walls—while taking immeasurable care not to hit the paintings—

and punch a few dents in the drawers. Glass shatters in the barrage of piling chips, and lost within it all, my enemy lurks. I glance back at the vase, now roiling with magenta light. I've got to act fast.

"Take this, you selfish prick," my assistant shouts.

I barely turn back in time to see the whisky bottle flying at my head and duck to avoid the crash of glass on the rear wall. I fly right back up, my blood pumping through my neck, my skin an itchy outrage.

"How dare you waste that premium vintage, you callous bastard!"

"Waste it?" my inferior reflection snaps back. "The bottle's empty, you dolt."

Outrage seethes into blistering hate. "Wha—And you call me selfish?"

I redirect my breakfast scroll with renewed bloodlust, bellowing curses amidst ultimate chipmageddon. My greatest enemy ducks for his life, and I seize my moment, snapping the scroll closed. I discard it onto the table and tear silver free from my belt, ready to end this once and for all.

Across the table, a bruised hand reaches up and slams onto the wood for purchase, my target peeking over the lip to glean the situation. "It's the bloody spud-apocalypse in here—Gah!"

I throw myself across the table with a murderous cry, my spare hand wrapping around his emerging throat. The knife plummets as we descend to the floor, my advantage hard won.

He tries to bat me away, but my momentum blows through his guard, his eyes wide with understanding. The blade sinks for his heart, unstoppable on its path, when a jag of agony stabs my mind.

Get out!

My limbs seize from the psychic blow stabbing between my ears, and we both collapse helplessly on the floor. The hardwood punches me square in the nose and hot blood pumps over my lips. I scramble for my fallen blade, but another splinter of fury impales my brain. Horrific images of an enraged psychopath ramming the tip of an icicle beneath my eye consume me.

I warned you, old man.

The hellish voice snarls deep within the folds of my mind. Each word drips with scorn. The demon's invasion squirms like a tadpole beneath the skin. Burrowing ever deeper and hungry to rend my humanity with vicious gnashing teeth. My legs kick uncontrollably against the squirm. I rake my fingers over my skull for reprieve, but there isn't any.

Fighting for control of my limbs, I claw my way towards the door, slapping and kicking at my fake assistant who is trying to do the very same. Visions of dark lightning crackle across the room. They fill my mind, setting the nerves in my back on fire. But revenge comes in a different form. As I struggle to rise, another volley of blistering pain kicks my legs out from under me, and the squealing side of bacon, running hot laps around the room, crunches the bones in my hand on the next pass. I bite my lip and pull my hand back in, in time to cover my head from a barrage of eggs. The path to salvation is littered with a delicious breakfast covered in dirt and dust. Fucking hell. Could this night get any worse?

Yes.

The word thrums with horrific intent, and a thousand psychic blades peel along the contours of my skull, locking me in a stranglehold that melts reality and inverts my eyeballs. I can't think. Can't see. Can't escape.

It feels like my soul tears free from my body, and suddenly, I'm tumbling through the hardwood floor into the blackest infinity I have ever known, spiralling into the depths of madness and despair, destined for another world. Only the feeling falls away as quickly as it came, and I realise that I am no longer falling, but standing on solid ground. The realisation plays havoc with my senses, but I've suffered worse in my time, and scan my surroundings for whatever may be coming next. Though I cannot see it, I can feel it. Nestled in the darkness ahead, something wicked lurks.

Like a rolling bank of fog drifting through the hills, a fiery lake fit for Hell itself bubbles in the near impenetrable gloom, the crimson light straining my eyes. Thick globules of sulphur and ash coat the air, released from the lake's depths to taint my soul. And before it all, perched atop a lonely rock, a slender form of blackest night resides. Its thin, vicious tail lopes back and forth dangerously. Almost... playfully. If only that were the case.

Uneasy, I step towards the dark form, my heart rising into my throat with every precarious step. For all I know, I could be walking towards oblivion itself. Never in all my years did anything match the raw destructive capability of this one soul. And now, after damn near a decade of silence, the sleeping demon has most definitely awakened.

The silhouette twists around on my approach, its golden eyes halo bright and burning away the swirling shadows, stealing my breath away. They burn like twin suns, glittering in the night and more precious than gold, beguiling the wrathful nature of that to which they belong. Like supernova in the sky, they consume all they touch with their otherworldly power... their beauty... their destruction.

"Why have you come?" echoes a familiar voice from across the black-rock shore.

Hearing her with my ears is strangely unnerving. It's a voice I thought I would never hear again. I search for the words to reply, but sense abandons me. Only the warm press of psychic power caressing my mind remains, skimming my thoughts. My feelings. I swallow, making to speak, but the demon before me vanishes, leaving me staring at the bubbling lake of fire, confused.

My spine tingles with warning, but before I can react, I feel the press of something behind me, and the soft thrum of leathery wings curling around me. The light is low, but I can still make out the lethal barbs along their ridges. The wicked tines atop their tips. Bladed nails encircle me, cutting through my shirt and painting my chest red with heat. Molten breath simmers against the nape of my neck, running my blood cold. Something else, burning hot, presses against the small of my back, sliding beneath the belt line. I see jet black horns emerge beyond my right shoulder. And hellfire eyes, incinerating me layer by layer, until I am stripped back to less than a man. Hot breath finds my ear, with words whispered to the backdrop of bubbling flames.

"You're welcome."

What? Before I can hazard the question, wings and claws retreat to darkness. I spin around, only to find myself alone once again.

Go. The quiet word echoes in my mind, tinged with sadness. Regret. Turning back around, I find the demon returned to her lonely perch. *Do not return to this place. You do not belong.*

The words are like a lead weight around my neck, and I find myself speaking without thinking.

"My stockroom?" I ask foolishly, feeling like the child before a grown woman.

It's my stockroom now. Remember?

That stirs something within. Hope? The hell if I know. I'm still getting over the shock of surviving this deadly encounter. So many things fight to leap from my tongue, jumbling into a hot, garbled mess.

Now go...

Before I can make any sense of it, banks of impenetrable night swirl to block the demon from my sigh. They usher me back into a free-fall that makes my nuts crawl into my stomach for protection all over again. The ethereal dark clouds give way to real ones, and suddenly I'm plummeting through the sky, speeding towards an empty patch of land, while shards of icy rain spatter against my skin. A dark building, nestled between valleys, rests on a hill below. *My* lonely hill. All the arm windmilling does nothing to arrest my fall and I brace for impact. I'm unable to tear my sight away as I pass unharmed through the roof and hit the floor with a soul-jerking stop. The weightless impact plays hell with my mind. It should have knocked the wind from me. Should have bloody killed me. And yet, despite it all, I find myself remarkably unscathed.

Scanning the room, I realise I've been dumped out of a scary world and into an entirely more bizarre one, where sausage-link fire and cluck-crazed chickens persist in an orbital bombardment of eggy proportions. Covering my head from the chaos, I see my backstabbing former assistant lying face down in the dust beside me, apparently also waking from a nightmare. We look at each other for but a second, only to continue our mad scramble for the door, my arse crack seriously on fire. There's no time to scratch it. If there's one guarantee the beast residing upon the mantelpiece assures, it's that there are no guarantees.

Scrambling full charge beneath a storm of sunny-side-up, we dive for the door, our hands landing atop one another in a bid for escape. We pull the door wide as one, ducking towards salvation with gasps of earnest relief.

"Night Mother be good," my double says, beating me to it. Bastard.

I double over to my knees, grateful for a moment's reprieve. It doesn't last. Before I can suck down a single sober breath, that second-rate drunk is giving me the side eye. They say there's no rest for the wicked, so why're they coming after me?

"You're dead, old man," growls my pilfered voice, the sound of silver ringing cold in the candlelit hallway. I look up at the twins brandished in bruised hands, his icy smirk an invisible stranglehold around my throat. When the hell did he get my blade? But I don't have time to ask. Once more he charges, the twins a blur in deft hands that aren't my own.

I snatch a candlestick from the nearby side table and throw it at him, but he deflects it with a metallic scream. It doesn't slow him down, so I grab the side table and hit him with that instead. Wood explodes into splinters, stunning him just long enough for me to unleash my wife's signature move. My foot flies, belting him in the bollocks so hard his boots leave the floor. He shudders violently. The blade falls from the hand that reaches out to grab me. He reels me in by my torn and bloodied shirt, so close I can smell the betrayal on his breath.

"Sh—She kicks harder." His voice croaks.

My own eyes light up, but before I can respond, he belts

me between the legs so hard it sends me reeling to the floor. In a desperate gasp of breath, my lungs seize while my balls disintegrate. He's not wrong. She was the truest ball buster there ever was. Shit, I can still see straight. Weak.

Chasing victory, my murderous assistant leaps down upon me, his blade falling for my chest in what can only be described as a serious fucking case of déjà vu.

I throw up my hands and catch his bunched fists, the spike of my demise resting heavily over my chest. I try to shove him off me, but his knees are planted wide at my sides, pinning me completely. I'm trapped.

"She spoke to me, you know," he whispers, the veins straining in his neck. Our hands shake with the struggle. "Told me you weren't worth a damn. That I should take your place. That you're not worthy."

Emotions ripple through me, sharper than any blade can cut. He carves a jagged smile, leaning his bodyweight deeper into my doom. My strength wains. I cannot dislodge him. He leans lower, hungry for the kill.

"What solace did she offer you in your final moments, old fool? You can tell me. It's the only thing I don't know about you, after all."

Defiance flares within me. If I'm going to die, I sure as shit am taking this obnoxious prick with me. I let go with my right hand and slam it palm first through the blade, screaming with magma seared rage.

He falters at my play, just enough for me to launch the fucker sideways onto the floor beside me, but it doesn't stun him for long. He renews his effort, panicked by the desperation of my final gambit, but I drive my hand against the hilt and hold it fast. The blood pumps from my hand. My fingers are spasmodic with pain. I slide my left hand down to the small of my back and grip the handle of something sinister poking from where my silver once rested, the hilt distinctly more demonic in design. I rip it free and bury it in his chest.

Shock and horror are painted across his wrinkled features. He kicks away, his silver clattering to the floor. He stares in wonderment at the malevolent blade that's drinking his blood, seemingly unable to believe it. He tears at his shirt, now bloody and torn like my own. Fiery veins spread across his chest like poison, scorching battle-worn skin to an ashen wasteland in its wake. Astonished, he looks up at me with questions on his lips.

"Wh—Where the fuck did you get *that*?"

I can't help but smile. I rise onto my feet to better watch my usurper meet his end.

"What, you didn't know?"

He shakes his head in disgust, his eyes beginning to roll and his hands burning to the molten touch of the blade. Pillars of smoke drift to coat my nostrils in charred flesh.

"She fucked me again," he mumbles, falling back onto his elbows. "Bloody... bloody women..."

Flecks of his skin turn to ember, rising on waves of glowing cinder like fireflies taken flight. "... you just can't live with 'em—"

He falls back heavily with a strained gasp, his limbs and face succumbing to the creeping flames, and, finally, breathing his bloody last.

"Can't live without them," I say, finishing for him and shaking my head. He isn't wrong.

Staring at the burning husk of my own corpse, I find myself not nearly as relieved as I had planned to be. It doesn't take long for the limbs and torso to crack, breaking apart in great fissures of ash. The blade falls to the floor with a metallic ring that is nothing close to what this world would consider being metal. Looking closely at the crimson fang, it dawns on me that I should be cinders, too. Ah—Her words flash across my mind, and suddenly I understand.

"You're welcome."

I consider the bloody mess that is my hand. Gritting my teeth, I draw the blade from my flesh with a wet suck that threatens me with a blackout. Welcome indeed. I let the silver join the other blade, so glad to be done with it all. Hmph. Wonder what that paltry handout is going to cost me down the road. Still, I'm alive, and my shop is in better shape than ever.

Outside the window, the first of dawn's light refuses to stir beyond the mountains. It's still a way off, but surely drawing closer than ever. This night is nearly done, and I cannot help but feel this has been a damn good night, all things considered. Also, I can't help thinking there's something I'm forgetting... I'm sure it'll come to me, whether I want it to or not.

For now, I need to get rid of this damn body. It won't do to leave it lying on my hallway floor for some snooping busybody to find. Mother knows when the Chain might come sniffing about. They'll probably call me the bloody imposter, knowing my luck. I've got to clean this mess up now. Maybe then, finally, I can make my own goddamn sale. Prove that son of a bitch just how wrong he is about me. But first, I've got to stash this prick before he starts stinking up my home.

I grab him by the legs and begin to heave, dragging him through the back door of my bedchamber and out across the wet, wind-whipped grass to the stables. Inside, the pile of corpses awaits our arrival, and I'm more than happy to add that son of a bitch to the pile. I chuck him on, grunting with the effort of lifting my own dead weight. As his corpse falls limp over the others, a sense of relief washes over me. A great weight, unburdened. He's gone now, and yet despite it, his words still hang heavy in my mind. I'm not cut out to be a shopkeeper. Hmph. But this night is not yet over. There's still time to prove the fucker wrong. It's a long shot, but that never stopped me before. I stare at the burnt-out eyes of the best assistant I ever had; almost sure I caught a sarcastic twinge on those scowling, dead lips.

"Not bloody likely," I mumble in his absence, the words sailing from my mouth as though they were his own. I grumble at that, staring down at what might just be the better man. As much as it pisses me off, the mouldering bastard's probably right.

CHAPTER ELEVEN

The bedchamber hearth snaps and crackles at my back, the resinous pine burning fast and bright in a bid to cast away the darkness. Outside, the rain falls heavily now from a calamitous sky, the ominous thunderheads flashing with rage. It would all be rather cosy, were I not jumping at shadows every time the candlelight wanes.

I flex my bandaged hand, the freshly bloodstained, punctured skin tingling with a dull ache. The astringent vines of Silent Goodnight may taste like a disconcerting mix of aniseed and dog's arsehole, but it sure does wonders for the pain. I spit the ball of herbs out, unable any longer to stand the gritty film coating my mouth. At this point, I would rather suffer and be done with it.

A scurry of claws pulls me around in my chair so fast I nearly fall out of it. I glance over my shoulder. Taking in what's behind me, I spot a fat rat darting into a dark corner of the room and out of sight. I tut irritably at myself, part for jumping at the sound of vermin, part for not yet having set down a trap. That fat bastard would be perfect for the corpse roses.

Black thoughts of sudden evisceration alleviated; I turn back to the desk. All is well, but for how long? The crazy man that no longer sounds so crazy irked me, and the old blood vampire had spooked too. In my long years of experience, it's times like this when you shut the hell up and pay attention. The night's not over yet, and whatever freaked them out has every chance of stopping by just like they did before it. Sitting here alone, it almost feels inevitable.

Thunder hammers above like iron on tin, shaking sheets of rain loose upon the world. It's black as pitch outside; the moon smothered by endlessly rolling storm clouds. Little more than orange flames reflect in the glass of my window. If I stare long enough, I see the glare of ravenous eyes. The ghost of my wayward assistant come back to haunt me. I try to shake it off. Tell myself to stop being stupid, but I can't help but feel there's more to it than an overactive mind.

A shade deep within the night drifts from my sight, making me rub my eyes. Something *was* there, I'm sure of it. Maybe just another customer. Or maybe my bell's about to toll. I lean back in my hardwood chair, drumming my fingers on the desk. Let them try. Many have before them and look who's still here. Let them creep through the shadows. Everything else does.

I sigh, contemplating the guttered candle on my desk, my tongue smacking against the roof of my mouth. So many damn candles burn that the air's thick with fat. I can feel it coating my skin, my tongue, my clothes. It sure beats an ambush, though. In all my years, I've never met anything sliding through shadows that I would consider friendly. Shrugging, I pick up a thin splint of wood and work it over the sinking flame. Nothing to do but stay ready and wait for the sun. Isn't the first time I've been on the doom clock. With any luck, it won't be the last.

The unlit tallow candle fights the rekindling for but a moment. A shiny puddle forms beneath it as the wick finally relents and takes the flame. I give the stick a blow and set it down, my gaze drifting from the stick's smoking end, across the table, to that stupid book. A book of my Order, so it appears. Could just so easily be the mad ramblings of a loon. Despite myself, I begrudgingly pull it closer, turning the page to reveal a hard-edged ink depiction of a man clad in heavy plate, his face writhing in anguish. He seems to be reaching for the heavens, with the light to his left and a flame to his right. I gloss over a passage beneath, muttering out a rough translation.

"*...awaits in the abyss of the silent storm, forever.*"

"Abyss of the silent storm?" I've heard that before, but damned if I can remember where. If Sil were here, she would know. But I don't need it. Brennan's goal was always to defeat the darkness entirely. A fool's errand, I now know, though it took me a lifetime to glean such knowledge. Without darkness, there can be no light.

"Ah—" I slam the book closed, the depths of my own heresy unnerving even myself. I suppose I should not be surprised. Indeed, believing in an unreachable ideal and knowing the truth of such things can be polarising. Still... I'm no longer the man I once was. I finger the silver around my neck. Silver I've worn for a lifetime. Should I even be wearing it anymore?

Tinkle. Tinkle. Tinkle.

"Hello?" calls a voice, frail and distant. "Are you open for business? The sign says open. May I speak to the proprietor?"

I slam my palms on the table and push myself up, the wooden chair scraping on the floorboards. Forget about saving the world for a better tomorrow, about slaying fiends and horrors of the night. I ease across the bedchamber, making for the hallway. I've got a new job now, and it's time to go to work.

The shop floor burns with the strength of the sun, candelabra drawn from the corners to spread their glow, an army of candles perched atop the tables and counter. I even brought out some extra torches for the walls, fireproof as they are. Lifting the partition with my free hand, I step onto the floor and glance across the room, seeking my latest customer. The front door is shut, the funnelled walkways between the tables empty. No one's here but me.

"Must've left already." I shrug. The door says open for business. What more do you want?

I turn around to head back towards my bedchamber when a whistling wind sweeps past me. The hairs bristle along my skin. Darkness spreads across the back wall, the orange flicker of the torches snuffed out one by one into smoking trails of grey, their afforded protection lost in an instant. Something, black as pitch, swoops across the now shadowed wall. A shawl of ebon night lurks amidst the dark like a shark swimming beneath the waves, trailing rime along my spine. It stops, as if to regard me, then dives back across the wooden surface, submerging beneath the flustered glow of the candelabra.

"Good evening," croaks a stranger's voice, a decrepit old husk.

My ageing mind takes a moment to process the dance, but my feet are well versed in the steps, wheeling me around to face the unknown caller lurking at my back. I hold my cane up between us like a sword, but it's no substitute for the real thing.

An old woman, dressed in a moth-eaten pale green coat, stands in the centre of the room. Partially hidden in the pocket of darkness, her wrinkled face is drawn back into a sallow smile beneath a nest of twig-riddled hair. Her lace-gloved fingers curl like fetters around a mossy handbag edged with lichen.

"Good evening." I smile back, lowering my cane, but never releasing her from my sight. I pass behind the counter and secure the hatch behind me. "Apologies, madam, I didn't hear you come in."

"Oh, that's quite all right, deary." She smiles again, revealing gaps in her brown and yellow teeth when she steps into the smothered light, her heeled shoes silent on the scorchwood floorboards. "You are open, aren't you?" she whispers, her words hollow, as though carried away by the wind. "The sign said open for business."

"Oh, yes. We are indeed open," I hasten to add, leaning on the sturdy countertop to take the weight off my hip.

She stands silent for a moment, casting her gaze with murky eyes across some of the wares adorning a table. So, I wait.

"Very secluded location, this," she says, continuing to browse with interest. "Are you all alone?"

Unfortunately. "I am. I prefer it this way. Far enough from people, but close enough to still get some customers."

"Business good, is it?"

I shift on my legs while smoothing back a stray hair. "Well, to tell you the truth, I only recently opened, so not much yet. Dribs and drabs."

"No one to hear you scream. Sounds lovely."

My fingers instinctively twitch for the silver sword tucked beneath the counter, hidden from sight, but I resist its call against better judgement. She hasn't given me a reason. Yet. "How may I be of assistance?"

"Oh, well, I was wondering if you had any Cadghar's Whisker, only I'm after three of them."

I raise my chin at that, details of the deadly ingredient soaking my brain like a good single malt.

"Cadghar's Whiskers, you say?"

"That's correct, deary."

"A rare thread from the devil-beast of the same name," I say slowly, taking a closer look at her. "You know, bestiaries have noted that the giant cat-like creature can turn a man to stone with its predatory gaze."

"That's correct." She nods with a glimmer in her eye. "But what they don't mention is that the victim lives for eternity, thereafter, watching from maddening silence forevermore."

Indeed, they do. But how would you know that? The only people I know with such knowledge are guild apothecaries and dark practitioners from the Everdark, and you sure as hell aren't part of no guild.

"You know your stuff." Now what would a little old lady want with such a powerful tool, I wonder?

A tingling pain stirs within my leg, travelling up to my hip. An itch I just can't scratch. It's been a long night. My old bones don't take kindly to extended stints out of a chair.

"Would you mind if I see before I buy?"

"Of course, I would have it no other way." I shift again on my legs, silently cursing this useless body. "Though I should warn you, the petrifying properties remain long after the whiskers have been harvested."

"Wonderful." She flexes her lace-gloved fingers over her handbag. They crack like heavy boots on dry sticks, making me wince. I don't show it. Never give anything away for free.

The old lady seems unfazed by the danger. No mere old lady, then. Was this who my previous customers feared? An assassin, maybe. And who's to say that she isn't here for me? I've made more enemies in my long life than any breathing man has a right to, and my profession didn't always aid those who shun the light. In fact, I was their bane. Will you be mine, old lady of the Everdark?

Casually, I shift along the counter, my fingers trailing the wooden compartments beneath until I feel the letter C engraved in the wood. Without taking my gaze from her pleasant visage, I stoop low, feeling for the rectangular box of ancient wood.

Nothing.

I dip down, gritting my teeth against the burn in my hip, while I stare into the empty space below the counter.

Gone.

I rack my brain. What the hell did I do with it? The answer dawns on me like a flicker of flame. Idiot. How can I expect to run a shop if I can't even...

I pop up to face the hag waiting patiently across the counter, her arms curled up, the mossy handbag clutched tightly to her chest.

"Forgive me," I say. "I just remembered they're in the back room. Would you excuse me for just a moment?"

"Certainly, pet." The wrinkles crease deeply across her weathered face as the sagging skin draws back into that sallow smile. "No rush. I like to savour the experience."

I hold down a sky-bound eyebrow at that before excusing myself once more and hobbling through the hallway to my stockroom at the back of the shop.

"Stupid... stupid," I whisper, dragging my bad leg across the room to the wooden dresser in the corner beside the dead hearth. What's the bloody point in ticking off inventory if you leave it lying around all over the bloody shop?

Frustrated, I yank open an empty drawer, only to wince

and glance back at the mantelpiece. The vase is stone cold. Dormant. Thank fuck. Easing the drawer closed, I pull on a second. A rectangular box of black dread oak sits amongst a mess of spare parchment and an empty ink bottle.

"Ah... There you are."

Relieved, I grab the black box and turn for the door, but a swirling glow of fire catches my eye, holding me back. The opaque stone of the chain-locked vase resting atop the mantel appears to bleed once more, its magenta contents swirling to the surface like smoke. The silver skull-shaped stopper's eyes burn with malice, a grudge left lingering to smoulder. I can almost taste the disdain.

"What do you want now?" I growl, taking a step closer. "I'm leaving already."

I halt in my stride, lingering on the ornate stopper, checking it's still securely fastened. Good. Last thing I need right now is that particular kick to the balls. I place my hand on the stone hearth and lean in close, studying the contents within the glass. Strands of magenta smoke coalesce into a tight ashen script, then flare into life, the words scorching against the impenetrable purple-pink substance.

"*Soon your bell shall toll... Arsehole.*"

The words disperse like burnt paper frittering away in the wind, lost within the swirling currents.

"Hmph." No love lost there, then. Honestly, you'd think demonic women would be at least a little less crazy... Or perhaps a little more? Unwilling to find out which, I turn on my heels and head back towards the shop floor, grumbling all the way. Hesitation finds me at the door, and I look back over my shoulder at the now dormant vase, its surface returned to stone.

"Bah," I curse, turning away. I've no time for your tricks right now, demon.

I head into the hallway towards the shop floor, finding the old woman gazing at a shrunken head on the counter. Wally, I think his name was. Oh, how the annoying has fallen, reduced to nothing more than a scribble on my stock list. My assistant must have put him there earlier, because I sure as hell wouldn't have.

"My apologies, madam," I mutter upon my return, raising the box for her to see and then placing it on the bloodworm counter with a hollow tap. "Had a little trouble locating the item."

"Oh, bless your soul."

The old woman chuckles, stepping forward eagerly, her squinted eyes cracking open to regard the black box.

"What a lovely piece," she exclaims, lurching forward faster than I anticipate, her shrivelled tongue wetting paper-thin lips, a ravenous gleam in her eye. "Carved from the living bark of the Dread Mother, if I'm not mistaken."

She drums her fingers on the counter excitedly while she tastes the next words, taking her sweet time before spitting them out. "Is it for sale?"

I offer a placating palm. "It's not, I'm afraid. Only the contents within are for sale. Dread oak contains powerful anti-magical properties, perfect for containing dangerous articles, such as these whiskers."

That this old bag identified it so keenly can be no coincidence. Potion brewers have used parasitic oak for centuries to contain their most toxic of ingredients. Perhaps she is active within the Rotted Circle, the vile collective of druids who skulk along the Dread Mother's merciless roots, harnessing the swamp's foul power to further their twisted beliefs. Though I doubt one of their number would be short of their own Mother's materials. They may lurk along the swamps and whisper through the trees, but many an unwary traveller has died at the hands of their corrosive craft. Nevertheless, I shall not part with such a tool. It is too useful to me.

I press the golden clasp that's holding it shut and slowly open the box, releasing a small cloud of stone dust that rises up and assaults my senses, exchanging the moisture in my throat for chalk. I cough and wave the air clear, revealing four silver whiskers nestled upon the sapphire-coloured cloth. Small cylindrical shells of stone lay broken about them like shed skin.

"What a handsome set of whiskers. He must've been a big tom," she says, rolling her hand forward, "Mr..."

I part my lips in a vicious smile that usually scares the village children half to death. It's the only one left to me after a lifetime of scars.

"Thank you," I reply, trying to ignore the now constant pain flowing through my hip, always baying for attention. "I'm known as the Purveyor."

"Ah, but that isn't your real name now, is it?" She grins, glaring up at me knowingly over her crescent-moon spectacles.

Damn right it isn't. Names are a dangerous thing, you snooty old battle-axe, and no one needs to know mine.

"I prefer to know with whom I do business, that's all."

"Understandable." You'll get nothing from me and like it. I shift my weight to lean on the table, my hip aching like I'd slept on frozen ground for a week. Really need to brew something for this. How can a shopkeeper be expected to run a shop from the back room? "The whiskers are two gold pieces each, but I'll do you the three for five. My treat."

She peers at me for a long moment.

"Oh. Bless your soul, deary." She then coos, opening her

lichen purse with a shrug of acceptance. "I suppose I can't argue with such lovely prices."

Her eyes flash dangerously, setting my teeth on edge. My muscles tighten like iron, and my heart and lungs pause their function in my chest. My whole body is frozen with indecision on what to do next. It's her move, but I won't sit idle. Silently, I claw my fingers at the edge of the counter in readiness and peel my eyelids wide. My eyes burn with the effort of not blinking as I watch her soiled glove slide from her mould-ridden purse. I curl my toes in anticipation.

I've got to be ready.

CHAPTER TWELVE

A BOUND CLOTH stacked with clinking coins slides from the mouldy old purse, hanging heavy in the old woman's soiled gloved hand. I immediately release a breath of stark relief, my clawed fingernails releasing their vice like grip on the edge of the counter. My imagination nearly ran away with me there. I need to be more careful.

Loosening the drawstring, she reveals the glittering contents inside. It's a fat stack. Fat enough to buy the whole damn village at the bottom of the hill from the looks of it. But from her demeanour, I had her pegged for a denizen of shadow resting along the border of light. Anything skulking within the Everdark doesn't much care for gold, relying instead on the barter of goods and services. Perhaps she's a witch then, luring men with promises of power, snatching their coffers to snag a yet bigger prize. Or maybe she's a ritual summoner dabbling with demonic entities. Maybe she was just running errands for her lord on his way to the fortress in Felgoth, but somehow, I doubt it. No. There's something more to this woman. I feel it in my aching bones, or at least deep in my gut, which could also just be the curse of an out-of-date bladder. No one does the courtesy of telling you that old age and pissing in the wind go hand in hand like coffins and nails.

"Was there anything else you needed?" I hasten to add, pulling a handkerchief from my pocket. Handling the whiskers with bare skin risks the petrification taking hold, and the supposed treatment for that... well, let's just say I've no desire to undergo such extreme measures.

"Ah," she says, making a realisation, the bones in her neck crunching as she looks up at me. "Some widow wax if you have them."

"Widow wax, eh?" The torturer's best friend. A rare by-product of waxen toadstools and silver widow spiders trading poisonous chemicals in a symbiotic harmony.

"The very same. Do you know the ones? They are quite rare, known only to grow in the south-western marshes, deep beneath the surface in the limestone drowning caves. They are quite lovely in the autumn when the rains are heavy. Have you been?"

"Indeed, I have." Though I would hardly call them lovely at any time of the year. The caves terrify and consume all but the toughest of old leather boots, but the toadstool's highly prized for its interrogation purposes. Once forcibly ingested—because I can't think why the hell you would choose to eat one—the fungus invades the host's systems like a parasite, taking control that it may feed, rather than having to absorb its host to survive. Chain it in irons and it can't feed, so you feed it instead; in exchange for the information in the host's brain. The parasite will drag the words from your lips, then eat you alive if left unchecked. A typical end for prisoners with a particular flair for pissing people off, though due to its dangerous ability to spread to multiple hosts, its use is seldom seen. Now, what would a sweet old lady want with something like that?

Her jowls draw back, like a wolf in a sheep's pen; the sadistic killer my gut is beginning to take her for. It's not my place to ask, and while the widow wax does contain curative properties, I don't plan on giving any product demonstrations. If I were a betting man, I would say selling such ingredients to her is a double-edged sword.

"Risky materials," I say finally, frustrated that I can't divine her intentions. "I don't just sell such wares to anyone, you understand."

"Then what's the point in running an emporium?" she counters, her fingernails hungrily scratching against her bag.

Indeed… What the hell, I'm intrigued. And what else do I have to lose, save my life? My curiosity piqued, I decide to take a stab. "Before I sell them to you, I must ask. What would you use them for?"

"Well, if you must know, I had a patient the other week who'd been bitten by a white widow. I used the toadstool to cure the poison before it could rot his brain stem."

"So, you're a healer, then?"

She pauses, her old eyes bottomless wells of knowing, the corner of her mouth tugging playfully. "I am many things."

I bet you bloody are.

Silently, I nod my understanding, my fingers screaming all the while to take up the sword. Of course, I've heard the stories. Others of my kind defy the odds and retire to old age, only to disappear for months, years even; their twisted corpses eventually resurfacing to bear the revenge of the world. Such a fate, I need it not.

Easing to my left, I reach for the cupboard on the wall,

refusing to show her my back while I peel open a door. A floorboard creaks like old bones beneath my shifting feet, and the earthy notes wash over me as I scan the various baskets of dried mushrooms that are kept inside, thirty kinds at least — most deadly — all gathered by my own hand. I snag my calloused index finger along the roughly carved alphabet in the cupboard's wooden frame, all the while keeping one eye trained on my guest's hazy reflection on the polished brass sheet fitted to the inner door.

The old lady stands idle, her tongue flicking, watching. Slowly the light behind me begins to change, darkening the blurred reflection of her skin to mottled ash, her eyes yellowing in their sockets, turning my spine to ice.

My fingernail catches the rough-cut W and I snatch the red-orange dogwood basket from its shelf, then spin around to my customer's innocent guise. The festering evil in her eyes is gone, the darkness nowhere to be seen.

I remember the warding hag stone sitting uselessly amongst the rack of potions in the back room, rather than in my pocket. And the vial of holy water that I topped up this morning, only to have left it on my bedside table, precisely where I can't bloody reach it. With my teeth clenched, I place the basket down beside the whiskers.

"How much do you need?"

She looks at the wicker basket, then back to me. "Three again, dear."

"They're one gold a piece," I warn, not taking my eye from her while I fish three from the basket and place them onto the worktop. "I can do all three for two gold pieces since you're a new customer."

She holds up the bag of coins. "That's wonderful, petal. How much do I owe you?"

"Seven gold pieces all together." A nice haul. More than nice, if I live to spend it.

Slowly, she works the drawstring open further and digs through the contents, pulling out a handful of golden coins, the origin of some I don't recognise.

"Oh, how about this instead?" She grins, her eyes narrowing as she places a blood-red jewel onto the counter, spinning it on its point.

I shift my gaze down to the jewel, a ruby if I'm not mistaken.

"Go ahead," she prompts, but I don't touch it. Crystals and jewels can be conduits for dangerous magic—more than a few of which have been known to contain horrific curses. Even the most restrained of the Shadowland denizens are known to be unscrupulous magic users.

"I can't take that," I respond, pressing iron into my voice. "Gold will suffice."

"What would you say it's worth in gold?"

"A hundred pieces, at least. A thousand, maybe. Who knows?"

"Well," she shrugs, bones creaking as she drops the coins into her purse and tugs the drawstring closed. "Consider it a down payment towards a prosperous new relationship together."

"You mean like a tab?" I ask, wishing to hell my hip would just fall off already and take the damn burn with it. "Listen," I growl through gritted teeth, longing for my chair, "I don't do that stuff. If you wish to buy something else…"

Naturally, I do *exactly* that kind of stuff. Barter is the major source of trade with such people, but I do so at my own discretion; *not* when it's forced upon me by an unknown entity. The wrong trade can make deadly seem merciful. There are too many stories in the history of my

Order detailing the disastrous consequences of befalling cursed goods.

The old lady scoops up the whiskers and toadstools in her gloved hand and places them in her coat pocket.

"Well, I suppose this time you'll make an exception for a stubborn old lady, hmm? Toodles, deary."

And with that, she slinks silently backwards across the scorchwood floor, whispering dark words I cannot discern. Shadows gather, welling into a pulsating darkness around her, her worn clothes and twig-riddled hair igniting with umbra flames and burn across her form with unnatural silence. The impenetrable black flames engulf her, reducing her haggard frame to a pile of dust on my floor, her wicked laughter echoing against the walls.

"The fuck... was that? And she didn't even put the whiskers in a leather pouch for safekeeping." Leaning on the bloodworm counter, I shake my head in disbelief. A long breath escapes my lips, and the room of dead candles burst into life, burning away the shadows anew. Some protection they turned out to be.

My gaze slides from the closing door to the red gem. The many planes reflect the candlelight beside me as it slows to a wobble and finally topples over onto its side with a *tink*. Shadows dance within those gleaming planes, or perhaps foul magic. I can't leave it here, nor do I wish to move such a potentially dangerous item. I drum my fingers on the counter, thinking... containment. For now, I need to keep it safe, so I retrieve a piece of black velvet cloth from under my counter and carefully wrap it within, then nestle it in my shirt pocket. Only a fool would touch that thing with their bare hands, and I'm no fool. Guess I'd better clean up that mess before someone slips through the damn thing.

Gingerly, I edge out from behind my counter and head

across my shop floor, taking up the broom resting against a table's end. I stand over the ashen pile, entirely bewildered. Did she die? Impossible, surely. It must be some kind of trick. A black magic of which I am not aware. Night Mother knows there's enough of it out there. Wondering if the whiskers might have survived the black heat—if indeed there was any heat at all—I brush the pile of ash to one side, gasping at the horror confronting me from beneath. Letters in a tight script, the words stark, engrained, and from the looks of it, completely irremovable.

"You owe me."

The broom falls from my hand. I drop to my knees and buff the dark lettering with my sleeve, praying to any god that might listen to save my pristine floor. With bated breath, I pull my arm away and stare at the polished words. They're more visible now than they were before.

"Nooooo!"

That evil, rotting, disgusting... bitch! I throw myself onto the floor, kicking my legs against the burning in my hip and flinging my arms about like every brat I ever wished to launch across the room for throwing a wobbly. I now know how they feel.

"It's. Not. Fair!"

I scream, rolling over and pounding the wood until my fists ache. I'm reduced to squishing my cheek against the warm wood in defeat. My poor floor. Tarnished forevermore. There's no way I'm buffing that shit out. There's no way...

My greatest fear in life now realised; I've truly got nothing left to lose. My shop is ruined. I might as well kill myself now. Nothing could console me. Nothing except... I lift my head, staring back at the counter, thinking of the entry left to make in my ledger, and the new totals of both my former assistant and my earnings for the night. That makes me smile, and I manage to force myself to stand. Crossing back towards the counter, I rub my hands with glee.

"Finally, it's time for the night's final tally." And time to prove who the best around these parts really is.

CHAPTER THIRTEEN

With the ledger opened to the correct page on my bloodworm counter, I find myself grinning like a lad after his first tumble in the haystack. I dip the quill in its ink pot and dab it on the side of the glass rim. Let's see here... Three whiskers and three wax widows sold by me. Sliding my hand along to the profit column, I pen the fat "100" below the other entries of the night. I'm about to add the "g" for gold when my hand freezes. Carefully, I relieve the velvet wrapped ruby from my chest pocket and peel back the folds to gaze upon its glorious crimson light. Turning my prize, it's impossible not to marvel at my success; irrespective of the odd snafu along the way.

"Well now," I shrug, adding another zero to the final number. "Not my fault I do good business, is it?"

I can't help but giggle to myself, thrilled to have smashed that motherfucker's total by a factor of infinity. Just goes to show I'm hot shit, and he was nothing but a steaming pile after all. I'll admit the sale was a little messy, but still, this thing must be worth a bloody fortune. Enough to see me through all the winters of my life. All I have to do is break whatever curse it's harbouring and find a buyer. How hard can it be?

Undeniably pleased with myself, I take up the imposter's mirror and gaze into its reflectionless depths, wishing he could see me now in all my glory. I nearly choke on what the mirror unveils. Not empty blackness, nor the abandoned stable's crumbling joists hanging precariously above my imposters discarded corpse, but a lone pane of glass dappled in rain, framing a sombre setting. The world within is illuminated in the reassuring touch of candle glow, and the familiar table studded with trinkets on my very own shop floor. Realisation dawns, sending my heart plummeting into my bowels. Beyond the dark red countertop stands none other than myself, peering into the depths of the damn mirror, the slow burn of shock's blade twisting about my old, weathered face.

"The fuck?" I slam the mirror down onto the countertop and whirl around to the adjacent window, where, lost in the consuming darkness, a flash of lightning reveals my worst nightmare lurking like a creep in the night. Me.

Lightning flashes again, painting my window view with the dead stare of my own reflection. I rub my eyes in the hope that I'm overtired. Overworked and clearly in need of a night off. Given that I delegated most of my workload, took a power nap, and only just opened the goddamn store for the first ever time, none of that seems particularly likely. I rub them good and proper anyway, squinting into the gloom to reconfirm what my heart already knows.

Much to my dismay, the husk of my own corpse still stares blankly through the window, its ashen palms pressing hard against the pane. When I said I wanted the bastard to see me now, I didn't bloody mean it.

"It was a figure of speech, you prick!"

My demented reflection shambles closer. The hilt of the infernal blade, still buried in its chest, presses against the glass. A spiderweb of pressure cracks radiate out across the window before it shatters beneath the strain. A cascade of razor-edged needles slice the greying skin of my stalker, and rain all over my nice clean floor. The body I just recently disposed of tumbles over the windowsill like a lead weight, eating daggers of glass with its abdomen and falling face first on to my floor, only to begin rising like a sopping wet revenant in the night.

"Fuck this."

Alarm setting in, I rush along my counter and drop down to retrieve the final word in every dispute I've ever had, drawing my silver sword free to kiss the cold air whistling through the breech. It is reassuringly heavy in my hand. My oldest ally and most stalwart friend. The enchanted blade is wicked sharp and unrelenting, its bite unmatched by anything I've ever come across before. In the end, it always has the last laugh. I honestly should've used it sooner.

Ready to finish the fucker once and for all, I turn to face my foe, stopping dead before the disfigured creature dripping red onto my poor scorchwood floor, nary an arm's length of bloodwood counter between us.

"Surrender," comes its emotionless command.

"Like fuck!"

Against better judgement, I lunge forward and vault across the counter. With my silver arching overhead, I bury it into the fucker's neck and chew through that filthy linen shirt, straight down to its blackened heart. My target falters from the bone-splintering blow, its blood and viscera spraying cold across my cheek. The mortal wound yawns wide, its burnt skin flaking like shed scales.

"The hell?"

The corpse sneers bloody teeth at me. "You'll have to do better than that, old man."

"Who are you calling old, you demented pri—"

The skin ripples around the sword, cutting my rebuke as I fight to drag my blade free. It slides from its chest with a meaty suck, the silver stained crimson with gore. Now it isn't to say that I'm panicking, but in my fairly extensive experience of making shit die, anything that defies the natural order with an injury like that can usually be categorised as seriously bad fucking news.

The traitorous bastard glances down at the grievous wound as though it were an afterthought, then raises its empty hand. "My turn."

I swallow, readying my sword for whatever it possibly could be planning. Fucker should be dead already. Fucker *is* dead already. Just what exactly am I dealing with here?

Another ripple distorts its mangled flesh, making me edge further back behind my counter. I would like to say I'm ready for anything, but honestly, how can I be? A hidden projectile, a leap of faith into the fray. These are typical outcomes, but with the way this is going, I wouldn't put it past it to shoot a bolt of lightning from its arse.

Across the countertop, weathered skin tightens and smoothes before my very eyes, although still riddled with blackened cinder and veins of char. Rent flesh knits a flawless finish, the once sagging muscles now fresh and full. Wrinkles draw back around its eyes and mouth, revitalised by the touch of youth. Even its hair, thin and grey only moments ago, is now black and full like the terrible night.

I stagger back before the chiselled form of another life.

A killer thought long lost, standing before me now like a window to the past. Only it isn't a window. It's a bleeding nightmare, and it's standing on my goddamn shop floor.

"By the Mother," I whisper, eying the strong jawline and that barrelled chest of tightly packed power. Gods, I was good looking.

"No," snarls my imposter, his voice an edge higher than before; that grizzled tone of a man in his prime.

The bloodied linen fades away, swirling midnight blue leather spilling from his shoulders, hugging him in a coat I lost long ago. My old hunting attire, its depths once studded with enough weaponry to take on the world.

"By my hand," he says, reaching his fingers up and out from the end of his sleeve, his empty palm rippling ominously like the rest of him. His skin draws into an amorphous shape that seems to stretch and grow to a considerable length above his head. The fleshy length tightens and refines, resembling something I dare not consider a possibility. With a resounding ring, the pale skin-toned object flashes silver, its edges bladed and fit to kill.

Fuck me sideways. "That's my bloody sword."

"Wrong," he replies. A matching wide-brimmed hat phases into existence to complete the look. My look! "Everything belongs to me."

His words fall with unnerving surety. A statement of fact that leaves me questioning my chances. I step back, enslaved to the malevolent gaze nestled in darkness beneath that wide-brimmed hat, his eyes flashing with a familiar hunger. For the first time in many years, I can feel it gnawing at my mind. Chewing on my confidence. Whispering seeds of my own destruction. An emotion I haven't felt in so long, I could scarcely recall what it felt like at all.

"I can see it in your eyes, you know," he says, each

heavily approaching footfall a tock on the headman's clock. "Can smell it in the air."

He passes through the partition to stand before me unhindered, his silver sword somehow far more intimidating than my own. He sniffs the air, his nostrils flaring to the dank and the must. "Fear."

"No." That's a lie, and I'll gladly take it to my grave.

"Yes. Fear of the unknown."

He steps closer.

"Fear of inadequacy."

Another step.

"Fear that you've lost your touch."

"We all lose our touch in the end," I say, rebutting his argument. "Pretend all you like, fiend. You'll never be more than a reflection of greatness, destined to live in memory's shadow. Perhaps you should try looking in the mirror yourself for once, you second rate knock-off fuck."

The scowl deepens, and before I can count how many nerves I've struck, my younger self is rushing me down in the enclosed space, his sword lurching with harrowing speed.

I duck a lateral swing and throw my back onto the counter as his strike impacts my poor wall. Then roll for cover with my silver braced high on the off-chance that he takes another shot. To my dismay, he does. The deathblow pounds my elbows into the bloodwood as my sword threatens to punch me in the face. I roll off, backing away before yet another strike finds me. He's bloody fast. Was I always so handy with that thing?

"Where are you going?" he asks. "Won't you fight to defend your precious shop?"

Fuck the shop. At this point, I'm just fighting to survive.

The real beast has awakened, and if I weren't shitting my skids with the thought of facing down the best I ever was, I might just be proud about it.

My pulse hammers beneath my skin. I upend the nearby table and send it at the oncoming bastard with everything I have. The torment of undoing all that painstaking organisation is numbed with an adrenaline-fuelled roar. I snatch up my sword and dash in its wake, baubles scattering across the floor every which way, my weapon primed to kill.

"Hands off my display, you bastard!" A flash of silver slices the hardwood like butter, splitting my defenceless table in twain. It catches me off guard. Gives him the edge. He darts between the cleaved remains and drives his cheap imitation sword at my chest with almost inhuman speed.

I narrowly beat the sword away with both hands. Sparks fly in a flurry of blows. Deafly screams of silver-steel echo against the walls. Had I a moment to breathe, I might be concerned that he's beating me back with one fucking hand. His raw strength is alarming, reminiscent of demonic power. My shoulders ache worse than broken bones on a cold winter's night, forearms burning hotter than the fires of Hell; but just look at the guy. Imitation or not, he's the real deal. No wonder people hated me.

I narrowly deflect another deadly blow, less confident by the second that his sword is anything but cheap. It hasn't taken a sodding dent so far, and if he hits me any harder with that thing, it might just be mine that breaks. A feat I would have argued impossible before tonight... No longer.

My opponent takes the hilt of his sword with both hands and readies another strike, so I cut my losses and turn tail across the room, flinging anything I can get my hands on back in his direction to give me some space to breathe.

"I said mind the fucking displays," he barks, surging after me with fire in his throat. "I've gotta clean all this shit up when you're dead, old man."

"Yeah? Then you're welcome to it." I grab a few light spears and begin launching them at the up-tight tosser. Only, he sidesteps them without a second thought and continues his advance, while my arm tires out faster than a teenager spying on his first milkmaid.

"Whoa!" I duck from a spear coming back at me, the razor edge whistling through my hair on its lightning pass. Perhaps it's not the best time to be reminiscing about simpler times.

Despite my attempts to slow him down, my youthful visage stands unfazed before me, a quizzical look on his face. "Going somewhere?"

Night Mother, be good. I'm really going to lose this. "You can have my shop…"

"I know."

"… over my cold, dead remains, you scum-sucking piece of shit."

"Tch." He shakes his head with a disappointed shrug. "And here I thought you had finally come to your senses. Ah well."

Rising dread threatens to consume me, but I never let it stop me before, and I'll be damned if I'm going to let it stop me now. I ready my weapon in defiance, taking up a sword stance that beguiles my intent. Only got one shot at relieving that sword from his wicked hands. Got to make it count.

"Very well," comes his unimpressed response. "Come and die, then. If you hurry up, I can throw you on the pyre with the rest before morning."

"With pleasure."

His foot slides wide in readiness, but I'm already kicking

off the mark. I shift my body weight low for a feinted sweep. Then bait an intercepting strike. Pivoting at a dangerously high speed, I adjust my sword to disarm the bastard and seize victory by the balls.

My opponent jerks sideways, running the length of his blade up my own and leveraging it upwards between the joists of the vaulted ceiling, disarming me instead. I watch in awe as my sword sings into the air, spinning end over end and landing comfortably in his hand. Bollocks it all. I remember that technique now. Too little, too bloody late.

He smirks. "My turn."

Silver cleaves at my throat, a hair's breadth from lopping my head clean off as I stumble back from harm's reach.

He pivots towards me, swords a storm that could reduce even the toughest bastard to a pile of mincemeat on the hardwood floor. Backing up sharpish, I wrack my brains for where he got the skill to dual-wield. I certainly don't remember *that* technique; and it seems like the kind of shit you wouldn't forget in a hurry. Bastard's been holding out on me. Wonder what else he's got up his sleeve.

Running out of room to manoeuvre, I turn and dash lengthways down the side of the shop floor and back towards the counter. I'm completely unarmed and out of options. Grabbing anything I can find, I throw trinkets and old books across the room in self-defence, only to hear each one be cleaved from the air by swords akimbo. Sickly potions pop in sprays of acid green and pustulant yellow, neither of which waylay him for more than a second. I reach the corner and spin around. The broomstick digs into my back as I press up against the wall, horrified to see him already standing before me, penning me in like a Christmas ham, honey-glazed and ready to take a spit up the arse.

He twirls his blades, stabbing one and slashing the other

down upon my head. I'm in more danger of kakking myself than ever. Hunching low and diving between my enemy's legs, I scramble for salvation beneath a chorus of thunderous strikes snapping at my heels. Desperate to escape, I bust free from the nether regions of my own shadow, more willing to have egg on my face than my own nuts any day.

"You're dead, you cretinous cur!"

Terror ignites across my skin, and I roll over to see my silvery demise falling like shooting stars. I roll left, then right. Pinned between equally horrifying ends with no escape in sight.

"Go fuck yourself," I bellow back at the handsome devil, hoping he doesn't take it literally. My boot flies, belting him in the bollocks with everything I have. I fight the urge to curl up in a little ball and cry on his behalf, watching the jag of agony rippling across my younger self's face as he buckles towards me, slack-jawed and eyes bulging.

Desperate for an out, I reach up and grab the infernal hilt buried in his chest, throwing up my legs and propelling off his shoulders, fire erupting in my hip and spewing from his chest. The blade grates free with a burst of sparks, staggering my foe backwards with a lung-trembling gasp. He falls to a knee as I rise, dropping a sword and clutching at the hole in his chest, scorched skin rippling like quicksilver. The veins of magma begin to fade, his skin restoring to perfect health once more. He glances down where the crater in his chest once lay, his soft laughter edged with relief.

"That was a particularly hot thorn in my side," he says, taking up the sword and rising to fix me with a devilish grin. "I don't know whether to kill you or thank you. Guess I can do both." He readies his swords, looking more confident than ever. "Thank you."

"Welcome." Now what? That kick to the jewels would have bankrupted most men, but I've imparted him with too much tolerance for that shit, all thanks to a lifetime spent suffering my wife's calamitous thighs. By all that is good, I hope she didn't hear that.

Blades whirl before me, a burst of speed reducing the space between us with a bone chilling pace. I do the unthinkable, throwing myself into his assault with the dagger held high, catching him completely out of position.

He tries to scrub off momentum, but it's too late. I catch a sword with my knife and throw it wide, opening his guard and stabbing for his black heart.

Desperate hands relinquish the swords, his open palms clamping down on the blade like a vice. A mountains cape of veins rise across his skin, his teeth gritted with the effort of halting the blade. I lean into the hilt with my entire bodyweight, but he doesn't give an inch. It feels like trying to ram a stick through a wall of bloody iron.

"Nearly got me there." He laughs, mostly from relief. His eyes widen suddenly, his attention on his hands. Spindles of smoke bleed from beneath his fingers, the ever-burning blade beginning to glow with magmatic intensity. Sweat beads his forehead, vanishing into a thick, dark brow. His fingers begin to tremble, the skin blackening to a brittle char.

"Grah!" He throws the blade sideways, and me along with it, nearly spilling me onto the floor. I whip back around, ready to renew my attack before he can respond, but the bastard's already gripping his fallen swords, charred hands rippling with renewed vigour.

"Fucking hell."

"Coming right up."

In no hurry to stick around for the show, I cover my bases and turn on my heels, clutching the piping hot blade like my life depends on it as I dash madly around the counter. I wish my life did depend on it. Then maybe I'd have a fucking option left to my name.

"There's nowhere to run," calls my own arrogant voice from somewhere close behind, but I don't bother turning back, instead dashing through the counter's partition and slamming it down in his face like any respectable business owner in need of the last word.

A silver sword lands heavily on the counter, scissoring to meet me. I barely duck in time, popping back up and grabbing at whatever the fuck I can to try to defend against a direct hit. I scoop up the bastard's mirror, holding it between us like I've got the answer to all my problems. And perhaps I do, because my murderous younger self freezes in place across the bloodwood. His face twinged with discontent.

"One move and I'll break it," I warn, holding the mirror's unblemished surface to the edge of the counter, the infernal blade poking towards him like a child's ember-encrusted twig. Just having something between us makes me feel immeasurably better. "Don't think I won't."

"Go ahead."

"Ngh? You testing me, boy? 'Cause I ain't bluffing."

"I'm waiting."

My confidence waning, I grit my teeth and slam the mirror's glassy surface mercilessly against the bloodwood edge, the wooden body recoiling away from the impact with a glassy *chink*. I turn it over, staring dumbfounded at the unmarked mirror. The hell? There's no way it could suffer a blow like that. Unless—

"Here. Let me try."

I look up, still half baffled. Then see the terrible arc of

silver steel rushing down to crumple me like autumn leaves. I swoop down, holding the mirror between us as I fall. The sword connects, slamming the mirror into my cheek and punching my lights clean out.

The dagger, idiot, echoes an unimpressed voice in my mind, cutting through the swirls of distorted colours clouding my sight. I try to shake myself off, instantly regretting it. Pain lances through my skull. Vomit-inducing images of spilling my brains all over my floor make me sweat.

"I—I can't use the fucking dagger." I snarl, drawing up onto my elbows. The world's spinning. I'm in no shape to fight.

Footfalls echo, looming ever closer, an umbral silhouette creeping towards me over the scorchwood floor. Death approaches, and I'm lying around with my dick in my hands, none the bloody wiser. My head falls heavy, neck straining as if a thousand ropes pull tight within my throat. I can't beat him. He's the best version of me there ever was. Maybe better still. The knife hurt him before, but even a blow to the heart wasn't enough to finish him off. The element of surprise is lost. What chance have I now?

Shut up and die, then, worthless old fool.

Looking up at my murderer standing over me, I can't help but smile. "She always was a callous bitch."

The new owner of my shop nods in quiet agreement. "Ain't that the truth? You had a good run, old man. Now, if you'll kindly die, I've got a business to save."

I fall back heavily onto the floor, the mirror and dagger loose in my hands, both my energy and the will to live spent. Her psychic words still ring uncomfortably in my ears, taunting me. Hounding a dying man to his last breath. What the fuck did she expect me to do, anyway? I am old. Said it herself. Bloody demon bitch.

Idiot.

I ignore the barbed tongue lashing through my mind. Watch the swords rise, hovering over me like a guillotine primed. I close my eyes.

Moron.

"Farewell, old man."

Virgin!

My eyelids ping open in a spasm of rage. I throw my shoulder sideways onto my right elbow as a sword slams down at my neck, missing by a heartbeat.

"The heck you doing?" My executioner snarls, surprised by my own actions almost as much as I am by her filthy whore lies.

"No one calls me a virgin and gets away with it." I lock eyes with him, expecting a bond of understanding, but he just stares back, dumbfounded, like I've lost the plot.

"What *are* you talking about?" But I can't answer, because something just twigged in my mind.

"Hang on..." I stare at the knife in my hand. At the mirror on the floor.

"Quit stalling. Your time is over, you senile—"

With nothing to lose, I ram the infernal dagger into the mirror, biting deep into another world and shattering its rippling surface into a spiderweb of inhuman screams.

Standing over me, my counterpart shudders uncontrollably, falling to his knees and grabbing his skull, his swords clattering to the hardwood floor.

"No!" he cries, slumping over me and clawing at my legs.

I sink the blade deeper, black corruption spilling from within and sizzling with an acidic hiss. I twist the blade, ramming it deeper still, in awe that something is actually working.

The surface of my younger self distorts with every twist,

while globules of silver wring into tendrils and he collapses before my eyes. Inhuman screams pierce my ears, dragging my attention to the mirror. A maw of hideous teeth stretches out, the once flawless surface withered like ancient skin. I rip the dagger from its silver hide, then stab the blade so deep into its throat I have to tear my hand free before the grotesque thing bites it off. Pollution erupts from its tainted lips, the wooden frame smoking charred black, veins of magma coursing through the grain. The accursed artefact shudders violently, its shifting body cooling to a petrified husk of igneous rock.

I look up at the handsome devil trying to replace me, only to realise it is now me who is the handsome one. Little remains of what once resembled me. The limbs and muscles have twisted into horrors beyond recognition. Indistinguishable mounds of warping flesh extend, bursting into a fan of writhing silver swords, their forms warping between mottling flesh and lethal form. Their tips angle towards me, ready to dice me into pieces. I cover my face with my arm, my skin crawling hot with dreaded anticipation.

"MiNe…" whispers the scorched horror before me, the face contorting beyond recognition, its voice a warble of distortion. "It wAs sUppoSed to bE—"

The voice trails off, its parted lips crusting hard and still. An eyeball stares out from a mound of burnt flesh, screaming silently until only a blackened sculpture of amorphous ash remains, the light in its gaze dying out like an extinguished candle, leaving nothing more than a thin trail of smoke.

"About fucking time, too." I edge back across the floor, out from under the monstrous hydra of blackened swords hanging over me. Only the real deal has survived, a length of silver-steel alloy lying at my side, its feint runes of power whispering for revenge. I snatch it up and lever it over my head, bringing it down with all the fury I can muster on that second-rate salesman son of a bitch. The blackened horror explodes in a cloud of ash, coating my lungs and my shop in equal measure. Limb-swords crack and crumble, shattering against the floor in thick plumes of soot. I choke and sputter, rolling onto my knees, horrific thoughts of cleaning flashing through my mind. He made more mess over dying than I did with all my living. "Selfish prick."

Wiping my lips on my sleeve, I stand and glance at the charcoal mirror before me. A quick stamp turns it to scattered dust, and I find myself falling back against the countertop with a massive sigh, every fibre of my being crying out with pain. I feel like I've been fighting a bloody war. And what have I got to show for it? The right to run my own goddamn business and wear my own sodding clothes? Woop-de-fucking-do.

Still... I carefully fish the ruby from my pocket, the night's events unfolding behind my eyes like a bad dream. The ruby reflects against the nearby torchlight, as brilliant as the sun, and probably worth twice as much. For better or worse, I came out on top. I made my sale. And I lived to tell the fucking tale.

Outside my window, the rain has slackened to a drizzle, and the first of dawn's light is finally shining over the Spinebreaker mountains. It's about bloody time, too. Pushing myself away from the counter, I cough a black cloud of soot into the dusty air. My lungs are in serious need of some smoke, and my shop is in desperate need of a good clean. Wonder if I've got anything in my stockroom that could— No, never mind. Think I'll do it myself for once.

I kick through yet another pile of dust now tarnishing

the memory of my once clean floor, fishing out the pipe from the ashen remains. Satisfied, I limp across the room to the front door, my pipe clutched tight in my hand, eager to take a seat and watch the world go by. I'll clean this mess up later. Because it's my shop. My pipe. And my bloody rules.

I can't help but smile at that.

CHAPTER FOURTEEN

My back hits the creaking rocking chair residing on my porch, bandages pulling at the raw skin of freshly cleaned wounds. The air is cool, not yet warmed by splinters of morning light peeking through the distant crags. Exhausted from my first night as a fully fledged shopkeeper, I wipe away the perspiration still coating my forehead. Clean clothes would be nice, but more than anything, I'm in desperate want of a bath. I stare at my bandaged hand, grimacing. Working that damn tub into the shop is going to be a real pain in the arse.

Down in the valley, a rooster crows its morning song within the sleepy confines of Glimmer's Reach, signalling the coming of night's end. The Spinebreaker cuts a jagged sky of golden light in the distance, as though you could reach out and peel away the murk to reveal salvation underneath. You would be a fool to believe it. There's no salvation left in this world; but for a few hours, there might just be some well-deserved peace. I stuff my pipe with tobacco, lighting her up with a blissful chuff. Smoke—the good kind

—floods my senses, the burning bowl stirring up memories of spiced apple and autumn leaves.

Reflective eyes across the fields wink out like snuffing candlelight as the creatures of the night settle down in their nests for another day. I, too, should be settling down. Never had much use for the light. Hides my enemies. Gives a false sense of security. No. The night is where I belong. But I can't see sleep finding me so easily today.

I drum my fingers on the wooden arm of my chair, while the blood red ruby burns a hole in my pocket.

"Bah."

Careful not to touch its gleaming surface, I fish the ruby from its confines and unfold the black velvet. Captivated, I stare into the reflective red planes. The ruby shimmers where there's no light to be gleaned, instead shining when the shadows find it. Curious. I turn over the intriguing stone in my hand, paying extra heed to keep it from making contact with my skin. Something swims beneath the surface, like a shark waiting to break the red wave and consume me whole. I squeeze it tight, scaring it away.

"Just who are you, old woman?"

Perplexed, I scan the dark fields all the way to the Everdark forest, my ceaseless searching bearing little more than rotten fruit. No mere old crone, that's for damn sure. Something tells me she'll be back before long. I can taste the dark energy radiating from within its lustre. Feel it in my bruised bones. This jewel wasn't meant to be used as a down payment. My gut tells me its purpose is far more sinister than gold.

A sudden wind catches me off-guard. A cackle nestled within urges my hand to snatch up my silver sword resting against the wall beside me, the ruby tumbling to the porch floor.

"Where are you, wench?" I growl, my hairs standing on end. "Come out and face me!"

Or, you know, just sod off and leave me in peace.

Slivers of the sun spear between mountain peaks, their warmth the gentle touch of an old friend, steadily burning the darkness away. The cloud's end rolls towards me from afar with a promise of blue sky, but that is all. The wind dies to a whisper, leaving me standing on edge like an old loon. It's all in your head, old man. Pull yourself together, damn it. Jumping at bloody shadows.

Finally, I put down my blade for good and ease into my seat onto the many bruises I've acquired throughout the night. Leaning forward with a groan, I scoop up the ruby with my aching fingers and hold it up once more to the gathering light. A distant thought worms through my mind. Something's wrong. Then it dawns on me. I lean over the arm of my chair and stare at the murky floorboards beneath my feet. The velvet cloth rests beside my boot, the ruby in my bare hand.

"Oh shi—"

Light flashes from deep within, an inescapable force tearing something intangibly precious from my very being. Swallowing it whole, its presence unknown until it began slipping away. A cackle of laughter echoes across the hills, drowning my skull as a vision of myself rips past my sight, the afterimage of disgust and disappointment written in the heavy lines of my own reflection. Black shadowed tendrils pull my other self into the depths of the red jewel, lost beneath its many refractions. It leaves me cold, and if I'm being honest with myself, a little frightened. I've had enough of doubles to last me a lifetime, but something tells me this is no fake. The disappointed lingers in my mind, stirring up a new kind of fear.

"Night Mother be good," I whisper, peering into the endless depths. "What the hell have I done?"

My trembling fingers find my brow, wiping the sweat away. I can't tear my gaze from the stone. A dark form flickers beneath the surface. Something ethereal. Something aware. The darkness shudders as if realising it's being watched, and I can't shake the feeling that I'm staring at myself; something in which I've become quite the expert this night. Stupid old fool. My assistant would never have made such a mistake, I'm sure. Thank the stars he's gone; else I would never hear the end of it. I fall back into my rocking chair, exhausted.

On the far wall beside my front door, a shadow slides along its surface, slithering silently away like a snake across the dew-dappled grass, headed for the Everdark. I blink, watching it vanish from sight.

"The fuck was that?" I ask no one in particular, feeling curiously hollow. Hardly the strangest thing that's befallen me tonight. Shrugging it off, I glance out to the horizon.

Shadows dance across the sweeping vista, the dark trees like needles in the night. High above, rain clouds continue their retreat. An ocean of stars dwindles, their backdrop of black velvet ebbing a bruised purple band to buffer against the growing strip of morning light.

Something steps over my grave, making my skin crawl. I almost throw the jewel across my hill and over the edge, never to be seen again. Almost. For some reason, I feel compelled to hold on to it. A growing need I cannot explain, or, dare I say, a dependence? Never should've taken the damn thing out in the first place. I might not know what it is, but I know a dark artefact when I see one. As for its origin or purpose, I can only guess at the plans of the demented. I spin it on its point in the palm of my hand, catching the gathering rays. It's a wonder I didn't rip myself from the mortal coil altogether. My top priority was met this night... I survived. Or did I? Anxiety nips at my heels, but I'm still here. What more can I really ask for? Only time will tell just how screwed I really am.

Another rooster chimes in on the morning song, dragging my attention to the village resting below the jagged horizon. The sun is reborn to the world, peeking over the mountain range to glean the horrors that await it on the other side, blissfully unaware of the grimacing moon sinking to take an unwanted turn in the grave. Already the fel creatures scatter across the land, hiding in what little darkness remains until the fiery orb in the sky suffocates their desires, forever ignorant of the terror lurking just beyond its golden reach.

Well, doomed or not, it's time to close up shop. It wasn't so bad for an opening night, all things considered. Kind of reminds me of the good old days, if fighting tooth and nail in the shit can ever be regarded with such fondness. Even made some sales, sort of. Blasted coins are probably fake. And I used up most of my good cheese. I take one last look at the ruby before stashing it in my pocket and rising on my sore knees.

"She was right, you know," I mumble to no one, shaking my head. "You really are a stupid old bastard."

Sword in hand, I edge across the porch until I'm faced with my door, the blood-tinted sign saying "Open for Business" taunting me. I flip it over to "Closed. Bugger off!" feeling a sense of relief.

At my back, the birds are singing, waking up to another day. I need to get the place ready for the next night. Idly, I wonder who—or what—might step through my door next. Stifling a yawn, I step over the threshold, more than a little excited to see what tomorrow evening brings.

Be it devils, ghouls or even zealots of the bleeding light, all shall be welcome at my Emporium of Many Things.

LIKE WHAT YOU READ? The next book in the series, 'Parasite Unknown', is available to order from Amazon today!

Sign up to Dan Lown's newsletter to keep up with sales, cover reveals and new releases! https://bookhip.com/WFTMMBP

Compassion is stalked by regret. Murdered by reality.

The world-weary and grizzled outcast knows the truth. Smells the danger. Yet the ominous arrival of mysterious travellers during daylight hours, seeking services unprovided at the emporium on the lonely hill, forces the Purveyor to make an impossible choice.

Worse, a deadly hunter cloaked in stealth and cunning has picked up a trail, closing in on the unsuspecting shopkeeper. Someone wants the Purveyor dead, but is that reason enough for him to betray his valued customers? Or will he hold the line and honour his conviction to shun the light?

Can the Purveyor survive a curse of good intentions, or will he succumb and join the horrors stalking the night?

If you find strange and exotic tales like The Witcher exhilarating, you'll be captivated by the intriguing exploits from *The Emporium Of Many Things*.

Order book two of The Emporium Of Many Things series from Amazon today!

ACKNOWLEDGMENTS

I would like to thank Donna Rogers from DLR Cover Designs for creating the covers for The Emporium Of Many Things series. You were a joy to work with on my first published series.

I would also like to thank my family for your unwavering support and for helping to see the fruition of many years work in the publication of The Emporium Of Many Things stories.

Thank you, as well, to you, the reader. I appreciate that you invested your time to read this book and hope you enjoyed reading it as much as I did writing it.

I would also appreciate another minute of your time. If you could write a review, no matter how detailed or brief, it would help other readers discover the story, too. It is a wonderful way to help authors to keep on writing more books and I am grateful for every review I receive.

ABOUT THE AUTHOR

Dan Lown is an emerging author of dark fantasy. This is Dan's first story for The Emporium Of Many Things series and is the 2nd edition.

When Dan is not writing, he is camping with friends, playing video games, and travelling to enjoy new places and experiences.

Sign up to Dan's newsletter to keep up with new releases and other news! https://bookhip.com/WFTMMBP

ALSO BY DAN LOWN

The Emporium Of Many Things series

Parasite Unknown

Demon Of Yore

Heart Of Stone

Prophet Of Nightmares

Justice Of The Chain

Tomb Of The Unknown King

A Glimmer Of Despair

Palace Of Broken Dreams

Halls Of The Unhallowed

Harbinger Of Horror

The Castle Of Wayward Shadow

The Death Of Thanatos Series

The Death Of Thanatos

The Madness Of Minos

Nemean Nightmare

Printed in Great Britain
by Amazon